T0116880

A QUEST FOR ADAM

by

Ann Gilbert

Order this book online at www.trafford.com
or email orders@trafford.com

Most Trafford titles are also available at major online book retailers.

Author Credits: "Sieg The Magnificent" was published in 1993 by Doral Publishing

This is a work of fiction. All of the characters, names, incidents, organizations, and dialogue
in this novel are either the products of the author's imagination or are used fictitiously.

Printed in the United States of America.

ISBN: 978-1-4269-6388-9 (sc)
ISBN: 978-1-4269-6389-6 (e)

Trafford rev. 04/07/2011

 www.trafford.com

North America & international
toll-free: 1 888 232 4444 (USA & Canada)
phone: 250 383 6864 ♦ fax: 812 355 4082

To all the boxer souls who have shared my life,
warmed my feet and warmed my heart.

Table of Contents

Chapter 1 -

Recollections

It had been several years since Sieg first made his arrival at the Wilson home. With each day he continues to work his magic, lending love, strength and character to all those who meet him.

Dan and Ellen Wilson watched their son, Scott, return to their world after a tragic accident left him, crippled, depressed and bitter. Scott had been a young, promising athlete who ran for the joy of running. Modern medicine would help Scott to heal physically but it was Sieg who led the charge down that path to recovery. Sieg healed Scott's broken spirit. From the moment he entered the Wilson's lives, his sole reason for existing seemed to be to please them, especially Scott. Their bond was unwavering. In return, Scott and his family had taken Sieg the Magnificent to their hearts.

Scott's sister, Kim, grew from a toddler to a young adolescent embraced by Sieg's special affections and protection. He was "Se Se" when she needed comfort or companionship. He was Silly

Sieg as he provided moments of joy and laughter with his typical boxer antics. Boxers thrive on humor and oh, how Sieg loved to hear Kim laugh!

Dan and Ellen enjoyed Sieg's love and appreciated a great deal the security Sieg offered their family. Sieg kept his territory and his human charges safe at all times with steadfast loyalty. An extension of their own responsibilities to their children, Sieg fulfilled his own duties at an effortless pace. His boxer traits, inherited from generations of boxers before him, made him an ideal companion. Sieg could frolic endlessly with Kim in the backyard, work diligently at Scott's side as a working dog, and lay quietly at Dan's feet as he read or cheerfully follow Ellen about providing her with his company as she performed her household chores. His presence was always unassuming; however, he was always there when they needed any of those things.

During Sieg's dog show career he made numerous friends for Scott and himself. His favorite mentor and veterinarian, Dr. Stockman, had ensured his contribution to the boxer breed with a thorough and responsible breeding program.

Sieg even managed to turn enemies into friends. Ken Adams, one of Scott's former rivals and tormenters was also changed under Sieg's mystic spell. Scott had grieved the loss of his best friend, Marty Spangler. Marty and Scott had been inseparable, raised from babies together. Marty had been killed in the same tragic accident that had cost Scott his legs. As if by design, Sieg had carefully weaved Scott and Ken's spirits together. Sieg helped turn their anger into respect and finally into love. Sieg accomplished this miracle, just like all the others, by simply being Sieg. No one would dare resist the charms of this big, loveable dog.

Throughout all of their adventures only one person came close to claiming Sieg's heart more than Scott. That person was Sally Anderson. Before Sieg entered Scott's life, she had been the only friend who stuck by Scott in the hateful world in which he imprisoned himself. After Sieg's arrival she, Sieg and the Caring Companions program accomplished the work that needed to be done. They helped Scott realize there was still a wonderful world awaiting him. Sally had stolen Sieg's heart.

Sally had stolen Scott's heart as well. Although they were both in their early teens, the bond between Scott and Sally grew stronger each day. If indeed this was puppy love they could have no better teacher in the ways of love. Sieg was their best example. Sieg loved without conditions. To give love and be loved were the only pursuits that mattered, an admirable ambition for anyone.

Chapter 2 -

A New Companion for Sieg

*S*cott started high school just shortly after Sieg finished his obedience title. Ken and Scott had finished making some necessary adaption's to Scott's new car. Ken, Scott and Sally now traveled to high school together each day.

Sieg was always perturbed on school mornings as he sat and watched his master and friends drive off without him. Sieg still went to school with Scott on occasion but his travels now were more limited to dog training classes at the center, a visit to Dr. Stockman or an occasional show just to let everyone know old Sieg was still around. At just a little over seven years of age, Sieg still presented a "magnificent" representative of the breed.

Sieg remained Scott's constant companion when Scott was not in school. Occasionally, Sieg was permitted to go with Scott and Sally when they started dating. He remained the school's mascot and was present for every pep rally and special event held at the high school. Sieg liked the outdoor activities best, like picnics and the track meets Ken and Scott attended. Ken, although not the natural athlete Scott had been, was doing quite well and Scott had signed on as Manager for the Track Team. Slowly he was learning to run faster with his new legs and although he could not compete in regular athletic events for now, Scott hoped to in the future. He continued to set his sights high and never hesitated to tackle whatever life had to offer. His self-confidence was as secure as his love for Sieg.

By far one of Sieg's favorite activities was going to the drive-in movies with Scott and Sally. That was wonderful indeed! Sieg could snuggle close to Sally on these occasions, sitting between her and Scott. Sieg would never fail to make a pig of himself over the popcorn. The two young teens could not have a better chaperon. No need to worry about them giving each other too much affection. Sieg demanded it all! Neither Scott nor Sally could deny him that affection no matter how hard they tried to resist Sieg's charms. They never considered Sieg a third wheel. Sieg was just Sieg and they loved him that way.

Each time Scott had the opportunity to see some of Sieg's puppies he found himself wondering if Sieg would be more content when he was left behind if he had a canine companion. Oh, Sieg still had McKeevor and John Edgar to play with but another Boxer would be grand. Kim was a good playmate, but she too was often busy in school. With his parent's permission and Dr. Stockman's assistance, Scott decided the time was right. Sieg should have a special companion in his life.

So the quest for a companion for Sieg began. The Wilson household prepared for the arrival of another Boxer. Kim was especially excited at the thought of having a Boxer puppy in the house. They had missed Sieg's puppy hood. The thoughts of having a little Sieg about the house had everyone excited. Choosing one of Sieg's puppies was the smart thing to do. Finding just the right candidate for Sieg's special lady may not be as easy.

Several months went by and it was nearly Christmas when Dr. Stockman phoned Scott to advise he had located a possible mate for Sieg nearby. The pedigree and the prospects were excellent. The female belonged to Amanda Nelson, a young woman who lived in Sieg's hometown. Scott remembered Amanda's name. He had seen her often at ringside during Sieg's show days. Dr. Stockman informed Scott that Amanda was willing to place a puppy with Scott in exchange for the stud fee for Sieg's services.

Dr. Stockman cautioned he would not normally recommend this type of agreement, however, in this case he knew Amanda Nelson was dedicated and sincere in her efforts to better the breed. Amanda had grown up with the companionship of a Boxer and wanted her future children to have that same special relationship. Her female was a champion and Amanda wanted very much to breed her to Sieg. Having a litter sired by Sieg was important to Amanda and her future breeding plans. If a puppy were not a satisfactory arrangement she would gladly pay Sieg's normal stud fee.

Scott could relate to that "special relationship" between master and dog as he listened to Dr. Stockman tell him about Amanda and her "special boxer." Amanda had closely followed Sieg and Scott's adventures in the show ring and the wonderful work they were doing with Caring Companions. Amanda was very impressed not only with Sieg's pedigree but his temperament and intelligence. Dr. Stockman arranged to visit with Amanda and her husband, Michael, the following Saturday. The solution to Sieg's companion was in view. Soon they would meet Sieg's potential "bride."

Chapter 3 -

Harmony & Sieg And A Sweet Melody

Two days before Christmas, Scott and Sally drove by Dr. Stockman's clinic and picked up Dr. Stockman for the trip to Amanda's house. Sieg was left at home, much to his disdain. Scott promised Sieg if things went well he would have a "date" soon. Sieg knew the word "date" so he was puzzled at being left behind. He sat pouting at the window when Scott and Sally drove off. This was Saturday, how dare they leave without him!

The drive to Amanda's house took less than twenty minutes. Scott followed the directions Dr. Stockman gave him with no difficulty. As they pulled into the driveway of the house Scott spotted a familiar form peering out the window, a Boxer. It was obvious she was trying as hard as she could to see who was coming up her walk.

When the doorbell chimed the brindle bitch darted out of sight. She barked only once. As Amanda opened the door, the bitch sat obediently at her side. The Boxer's tail was wagging as fast as it could. She was anxious to make her acquaintances but she still waited for Amanda to release her from her stay.

Amanda introduced her husband, Michael. Harmony made her own introduction after Amanda released her from her sit stay with the word "free." The mahogany brindle bitch was indeed a charmer. She quickly won Scott and Sally's hearts. What a perfect match for Sieg.

Amanda presented a copy of Harmony's pedigree. She, Michael and Dr. Stockman talked about the possibilities this combination may produce. All Scott could think of was having a puppy at home with this lovely bitch's eyes. Harmony's eyes were dark, almost black, and her rich black mask and slight white wishbone on her face gave her a devilish look. It was easy to see after only a few minutes that Harmony was indeed a little "imp." Yet her temperament was excellent. Dr. Stockman always stressed the importance of temperament to Scott. Harmony obviously possessed those special Boxer qualities, sensitive, affectionate and fun loving.

Michael and Amanda shared their plans to eventually build their own line of Boxers. They were delighted with the opportunity to breed Harmony to Sieg. Everyone agreed the match was to be a perfect "harmony." Final arrangements were made. Harmony would visit Sieg in a few days after a checkup by Dr. Stockman and the results of the necessary testing were received. It was obvious that Harmony was healthy and fit. Scott knew Dr. Stockman always made absolutely sure that both Sieg and his ladies were 100% before any breeding took place.

Scott returned home later in the day and told Sieg he had just found him the "perfect" lady. Sieg was still upset for being left. He just sighed and put his head in Scott's lap. He poked at Scott with his paws demanding the extra attention he knew he deserved. He was not interested in what Scott was actually saying to him, he just wanted to hear the sound of Scott's voice, to feel his hands stroking his head. He would forgive Scott but it would take a lot of this attention to make things right.

Two days after Christmas Harmony arrived at Scott's house for her "date" with Sieg. Amanda brought Harmony and. Dr. Stockman was on hand to see that the special event went just right. Sieg was delighted with his lady. The courtship was soon a love affair. Now the waiting game began, all going well the puppies would arrive the end of February.

On February 28th Amanda phoned with the news, the puppies had arrived, two males and three females. Amanda was elated. Two of the puppies were fawn like Sieg. Three were brindle like their mother. Best of all Amanda exclaimed was the outstanding fawn male, there was no doubt who his father was, and Sieg had outdone himself. Amanda said she would call the puppy Adam, as he would be the first of Amanda's new line just as Adam had been the first man. The brindle male she would call Shane. The three girls she had christened Abby, Katie and Melody. One brindle girl, Melody, Amanda told Scott was a duplicate of her mother.

Scott was delighted with the news. Sieg and his Harmony had made the perfect "Melody." Sight unseen Scott knew Melody would be his pick. Scott had decided early that he wanted to have a Sieg daughter. It sounded like Melody was made to order. Scott asked Amanda if he could visit when visitors were permitted. Dr. Stockman would dock the puppy's tails and dewclaws in a few days. Scott would wait for word from Amanda before arranging a family visit to the new babes.

An extra helping in his bowl for dinner that night pleased Sieg. He didn't quite understand the excited conversation around the dinner table. Sieg, never one to look a gift horse in the mouth, took his natural advantage. He savored the extra feed and extra hugs that flowed so freely.

Chapter 4 -

The Magic Litter

*I*t seemed like months before the puppies were ready for visitors. Finally the okay came and Scott, Sally, his parents and Kim made the drive to Amanda's house for the visit. Sieg would have to wait until much later to visit his new family. Harmony was still not receptive to canine visitors just yet, not even one as special as Sieg. Her protective nature was completely normal. The puppies were three weeks old and she was more comfortable with human visitors.

Scott peeked in the whelping box and Harmony raised her head to see who was about to look in on her little ones. Seeing Scott's friendly face, she wagged her tail and permitted him his first peek. The puppies were all lined up in a row suckling on their mother. It was dinnertime. Although Dr. Stockman had already told Scott that the litter was exceptional, Scott was not prepared for the beautiful babes before his eyes.

Adam, of course, stood out first. Amanda was right there was no denying his father. Katie was a lovely fawn. She was smaller than the rest but she took no back seat at the chow line. Abby, Shane and Melody were the remaining puppies, all brindle like their mother, just as Amanda had described.

Melody was a carbon copy of her mother. Scott beamed. "Your right, Amanda, Melody is just like Harmony. Adam is his father's son. I think we both came out with our perfect puppy." Amanda nodded in agreement as she reached down and picked up Melody and handed her to Scott.

Scott took the wiggling puppy in his hands and his eyes shown bright with appreciation for this perfect little creature. Melody's eyes were large and dark, like her mothers. She gazed at Scott with wonder.

Kim could hold back no longer. She knelt down beside Scott. Scott held Melody up to Kim's face. As the puppy nuzzled her ear Kim giggled, "Oh Scott, she's beautiful. Can I hold her?" Amanda nodded her agreement. Scott handed Melody to Kim. Now it was Kim's turn to beam. "Oh, Melody, we shall all love you very, very much. You will be my special girl just like Sieg is Scott's special fellow."

Amanda then reached down and picked up Adam. "And here my dears is my special fellow." Adam wiggled and squirmed in her hands. He had not finished his dinner and was indignant at this interruption. Everyone laughed at him. Amanda quickly placed in back in the box. "Just like his father, don't get between him and his food!"

Sally's favorite was Katie. Michael admitted that his favorite was Abby. Amanda and Michael had agreed to keep two puppies out of the litter, Adam and Abby. Shane would live with Dr. Stockman. After all these years, Dr. Stockman had decided that he would have his own Boxer again. Shane, like Adam, possessed many good qualities of both his parents. Katie would go to live in California with a dear friend of Amanda.

Now all that remained was allowing the puppies to grow and thrive with all the love that surrounded them.

Finally at eight weeks of age, Melody made the trip to the Wilson house. Sieg welcomed the new comer at first with an arrogant air. After only a few minutes Melody played the right tunes and she and her father frolicked together on the floor. Sieg rolled over on his back as Melody playfully chewed on his jowls. Sieg loved it! From that moment they were a perfect pair.

That night Melody slept snuggled in Kim's bed. Sieg kept a vigil through the night, leaving Scott's bed several times during the night to check on his newest charge.

As planned, Adam and Abby remained with Amanda and Michael. Katie had an exciting plane ride to her new home in California and Shane went to live with Dr. Stockman.

As the puppies grew and each began their show careers it was obvious to those on the show circuit it would be sometime before the likes of this litter would be seen again.

Harmony and Sieg's litter produced five champions but the star of the litter by far was Adam. Adam would carry on his father's legacy to improve the breed.

Besides having a beautiful companion for Sieg, Scott also appreciated the friendship he developed with Amanda and Michael Nelson. Scott and Sally shared many good times with them. When Amanda and Michael announced the upcoming birth of their own offspring no one was happier than Scott. When Michael was assigned to Germany with his Air Force duties, Scott promised he would look after Amanda and her growing brood until Michael's return.

Amanda was very much the independent lady but she promised Michael should she ever need help she would welcome Scott's offer. When Michael's plane left for Germany a few weeks later Amanda had no idea of the changes that would occur in her life. In just the next few months, she would need not only Scott's assistance and strength but also the compassion of people she had yet to meet. Adam was about to lead her on an adventure she would never forget.

Chapter 5 -

Flight for Life

The smells were horrible. The building was dark and damp. Only a small ray of sun from a crack in the door cast any light on the dismal surroundings. Chained in a corner just beyond the beam of light a dog lay shivering. He laid in the dirt, mire and his own body secretions. Close by, just within reach, were two pans. One was filled with stagnant water; the other with what remained of the foul food the dog had been offered the night before.

The dog moved into the shaft of light and one could distinguish his form and color. He was muscular in build with a red fawn and white coat. The fawn coat was scared and covered with blood and flesh, fresh from a recent encounter. The white of his coat was a dingy gray and stained with blood. A noise outside the building brought the dog to attention. As he collected himself, it was obvious even in the dim light that the dog was a proud animal. Despite his condition or surroundings the dog stood with a regal dignity to face whatever lay beyond the door.

The noise the dog had heard was the slamming of a pickup door. The dog recognized the sound. Several times in the past few weeks he had heard this sound as he spent his days confined in this "home." The dog knew what was to come. His body quivered with fear, anger and some anticipation. Perhaps this time his mistress would be on the other side of the door and not the humans who now made his life so miserable.

The door swung open. The full light of the sun caused the dog to turn away. His eyes were not accustomed to the light. As his eyes adjusted he could see the men standing before him. His heart sank. His body quivered even more with fear. The humans were the same men who had brought him to this hell.

The bigger human had a foul smell of tobacco coming from his mouth. The dog could smell it as the man reached out and unhooked the chain that held him captive. When the dog shrank back in fear, the man yanked the dog into the air. He let him dangle from the collar and chain. As the dog struggled for air, the man dropped him to the ground, "Maybe that will settle you down your big mutt!" The man then turned and forced the dog to follow. As they emerged in the full sun light the dog's breed was now obvious. He was a boxer. It was Adam!

Adam whimpered as he was dragged to the back of the pickup truck. He hung back as he spied the wire cage in the bed of the truck. He knew all to well what would follow, another long ride over bumpy dirt roads. At the end of the ride another night of fighting for his life. Adam's breed had been bred to serve mankind, not for the amusement of cruel, heartless men who enjoyed pitting dog against dog.

These men were the men who gave the name "pit bull" its shameful history. They bred and stole dogs for no other reason than to pit them against one another in a ring of fear. The participants were pitted against each other in battles to the death. It was no wonder Adam quivered and shrank away from these men.

Things had not always been like this, his memory of man was not all of fear hate and anger. Adam remembered love. The love from a mistress who thought the sun rose and set on him.

A yank on the chain brought Adam back to reality, no time to dream of days gone by now. The big man turned his back on Adam to unlatch the gate of the cage as he prepared to place Adam in the truck. While dangling Adam from the collar and chain, the man had not realized that the collar had slipped further up on Adam's neck. As he yanked the dog to bring him closer, Adam chose that moment to again resist the collar and chain. In that instant the collar slipped from his head. Adam was free! Adam's first instinct was to run. He barely escaped the man's grasp as he lunged to retrieve him. Adam took to the nearby woods, running, fleeing for his life. He could hear the men yelling and shouting behind him. He did not look back. Adam just ran faster and harder.

Weakened and hurt, he was not as fast as he could have been but he was still nimble enough to escape the two men who pursued him. The sun would be setting soon and the cover of darkness also would aid him in his escape.

Soon the shouts of the men were further away and Adam knew he was free of them. He would not fight for them this night.

The last shaft of sun fell behind the distant hills and the darkness allowed Adam to slow his pace. He finally stopped to rest in a ditch close to a small stream running through the woods. He was very thirsty. He drank the cool, fresh water as his sides heaved. His lungs labored to take in enough air to sustain him. He finished his drink. He was careful not to take in too much although his thirst was great. The water refreshed him a little. He lay down in the ditch. He was exhausted yet enthusiastic at his new found freedom. Adam could rest here for now but he knew that he must move on as soon as his body could regain its strength. The men who chased him could still be out there looking for him.

Adam licked his most recent wounds and tried his best to clean his paws of the blood and grime. In his race to escape the men he had run through more mud and water. While standing in the stream the worst of the grit and grime had begun to wash away. He finished with his task and Adam then rested on his side. He allowed himself to sleep. Adam slept fitfully. This was the first real rest he had taken since he had been snatched from the yard of his mistress. Just before Adam went into a deep sleep he had pictured her face in his mind. He could almost hear her soft voice calling to him.

The first lights of dawn found Adam again on his feet traveling through the woods. Adam was not yet sure of his destination. He only knew that he must find his mistress. He must get home before those awful men could catch him and take him back to hell.

In the light of day, no longer confined in the dank, dark building, Adam began to survey the area. He tried to get his sense of direction. Where was home? Adam topped the hill before him and gazed out into the valley below.

This was rural farm country. Adam could see cattle in the fields and some distance ahead there was a farmhouse. Adam once would have cheerfully run to the house full of the possibility of encountering humans. Now after the past several weeks of torment, he feared humans for the first time in his life. The humans at this house may be like the cruel men from whom he had just escaped. He would approach with caution. He would avoid being caught again. The cruelty of the men had made him wise. Not all humans were friends, as he had once believed.

Adam made his way slowly to the farm. He kept a watchful eye for men and pickup trucks. A short distance from the farmhouse he stopped behind a small metal shed. So far he had seen no signs of humans.

Unexpectedly Adam heard laughter. It was a small human's laugh. As he peered around the shed, he strained to see whom this laughter was coming from. There before him splashing in a swimming pool he saw a small human child. The little girl was perhaps three or four. Adam froze in his tracks as the little girl spotted him. "Hi, doggie" she called.

Children had always been Adam's favorite humans. They were small, soft to the touch and always smelled so fresh and new. His first instinct was to run to the child. Adam's tail wagged just a little. It was the first time the tail had wagged since the day he last saw his mistress. His suspicion and fear, however, would not allow him to follow his instincts. This could be a trap. The child could be bait to lure him back into the hands of those horrible men. The little girl called, "Here, doggie, come here doggie."

Oh how he wanted to go to feel her gentle touch. His body trembled, not with fear this time, but with expectation of a sense he struggled to recall and to relish. Adam's fear gave way to intrigue. He approached the child in the pool. Whatever the misery he had been through, this small child had not been one of his tormentors. She reached out to touch him. Her soft little hand touched his muzzle. Adam erupted into a mass of wiggles. The girl's laughter only increased his joy. He had forgotten the pleasure of a soft touch. This was not home, it was not his mistress. It was the closest Adam had been to heaven in many days. His joy was short lived.

Adam bounced about the pool and at one point he glanced to the back door of the farmhouse. Standing there in the doorway was a woman holding a stick (having never seen a gun, Adam had no way of knowing what kind of stick this woman really carried). Adam again froze in place and cocked his head as the woman spoke.

"Beth, get out of the pool very slowly and come to Mommy." The girl answered, "What's the matter, Mommy, he's a very nice doggie, he wants to play with me." "Beth, get out of the pool and come to the house," the woman now shouted.

The shout made the girl start to cry. The sound of anger in the woman's voice brought back Adam's fears. He turned to run. At the same instant, he heard the sound of a loud bang.

The little girl screamed, "Mommy, don't shoot the doggie. He's a nice doggie!"

For an instant Adam wanted to go back. He wanted to comfort the crying child. His instincts to preserve his own life were stronger. He continued to run.

Fortunately for Adam the woman had been a poor shot. The bullet had found a place in the side of the shed rather than the side of Adam's head. Adam had no way of knowing that the woman had simply been protecting her young from a large stray dog. A dog she had assumed from the scars and bloodied coat had been savagely involved in some sort of horrible battle. A battle, which may or may not have involved humans. Her child could have been only minutes away from death. She had driven away this threat to her little girl's life in the only way she knew.

Adam could still hear the child's cries as he topped the hill on the other side of the valley. The world was crazy! Adam was sure of it! Surely his mistress would offer him safety away from this world.

Adam traveled away from the farm the rest of the day. He carefully avoided any more contact with any farms, roads or humans. Adam headed west, a direction that seemed to call him. This direction left the cruel men and the farmhouse far, far behind.

As he traveled, hunger began to gnaw at his stomach. It had been almost forty- eight hours since he had forced himself to eat the retched offering his human captors had offered him. He could not keep up this pace or his journey without nourishment. He had found water in streams and ponds along his trail but his craving for food was great. Food was something even the cruel humans had furnished. For the first time in his life Adam had no one to provide him with something to eat. As much as he hated the thoughts of approaching humans, this urge would force him to consider this very approach to obtain what he desperately needed. The instincts to hunt and kill in the wild were long dead in this dog. He was a domesticated animal without the benefit of the skills to obtain game on his own. Oh Adam had stolen food before by mischievously getting into his mistress's trash or by stealing a cookie or piece of inviting foodstuffs from the table or kitchen counter. This situation was not a game. His abilities would now mean survival! As the day turned to night, Adam's appetite intensified.

The end of his second day of freedom left him on the outskirts of a small farming town still traveling west. He was confused, tired and very famished. Adam approached the town from the east the sun setting before him. It would be completely dark soon. He would take the time before dark to rest and contemplate where his dinner would appear. He found shelter in an alley near an auto garage. There behind some boxes Adam would wait for the safety of darkness to protect him. When the darkness finally fell, Adam urged himself on looking for signs of food. He was suddenly startled by a low growl. Adam pivoted in the direction of the growl.

A large German Shepherd stood chained on the other side of the auto garage. Adam had no desire to fight, although he knew how to fight and fight well. Adam had survived savage battles in the "pit." His captors had seemed to admire this ability to fight. On fight nights Adam had been rewarded with a taste of raw meat. This gesture was the only form of kindness the men had ever expressed.

Tonight, there was no one there to reward him to fight this dog. What was that just beyond the dog, next to his doghouse? A pan of food.

Would Adam fight? Could Adam fight this dog for the food in his dish? Adam seemed to consider his options. No he would not fight this dog for food. Fighting may bring the men he feared. There must be another way?

Adam knew full well the chain held the Shepherd securely. He was safe from the Shepherd's reach. All Adam needed to do was to maintain the distance between him and the range of freedom the dog's chain allowed.

Adam had also stolen food from his canine companions, even his own mother. Unlike his mother and littermates, this dog was not his patient mother or siblings. This dog must be considered an enemy. Still, stealing seemed more logical than fighting. He sat for a long while, surveying the area and the Shepherd pacing back and forth. Adam calculated the distance of the dog's chain and the exact location of the food in his mind. The chain was hooked to a pole near the doghouse, not to the dog house itself. Another pole stood between the first pole and the two dogs. Adam's mind continued to scheme. If Adam could somehow shorten the chain at the end attached to the dog, the Shepherd would not be able to make it all the way back to the house. The Shepherd's meal sat as a tempting trophy, waiting to be eaten. How to get the Shepherd tangled around the second pole was the question? It would be dangerous and timing would be most important. If Adam got the Shepherd to chase him, dragging the chain with him around the pole, it just might work. The danger was that the Shepherd might catch him first. If that happened Adam would have no other choice. He would fight. The first way presented a better choice; the danger was a worthwhile risk.

Adam moved to the end of the dog's chain, close to the pole. He cautiously placed himself just on the other side of the pole and purposely stepped into range of the Shepherd's reach. When the Shepherd charged, Adam darted to the other side. The plan was working. The Shepherd and Adam were now situated on the other side of the pole. A few rings around and the trap would be sprung. Adam again deliberately put himself in the Shepherd's range. As the Shepherd charged again, Adam ran circles around the pole. The Shepherd chased close at Adam's heels.

It worked! With just a few circles, the Shepherd had tangled the chain around the second pole sufficiently enough. He could no longer return to his house. Adam walked over to the unprotected bowl and feasted himself on its contents.

When Adam had finished and left, the Shepherd was still barking, crying and straining to free himself from his predicament. Adam was almost completely out of sight when the garage owner stuck his head out the door to quiet the commotion. He spotted Adam running off and yelled after him, "Get out of here you mutt!" He then turned to untangle the Shepherd mumbling to himself, "stupid dog."

The Shepherd would do without his dinner tonight. It was obvious that his sleek coat and extra fat would allow him to miss this meal with no real harm done. Only his pride was hurt, he had been outfoxed by this stray.

With his belly full of good food for the first time in weeks, Adam directed his search for a place to sleep for the night. He needed a safe place away from the noise and commotion he had left behind at the auto shop. On the other side of the town he found an old dump. There he discovered some old barrels lying about. Adam chose one that allowed him a good view of his surroundings. He was ever watchful for the men who chased him. Satisfied he was alone, he settled in for the night. Tomorrow Adam would continue his quest to find his mistress.

Chapter 6 -

Amanda's Horror

*J*ust a few days after Michael's departure Scott received a frantic call from Amanda. "Scott, Adam is missing!"

Scott listened in shock as Amanda described the day's events. The day started completely routine. She had only left the house only for thirty minutes to pick up some dog food at the local feed store. Amanda related that Adam had been reluctant to go with his sister and mother and her. It was a lovely day and Adam had been so content resting beneath his favorite shade tree. Amanda had given in to Adam's serenity and left him alone in the fenced yard while she, Harmony and Abby went for the dog food. The gate had been locked and she was positive Adam would be safe. Upon her return the lock on the gate had been broken, the gate was left swinging open and Adam was gone! Amanda had walked the neighborhood several times. Adam did not respond to her calls. Adam was nowhere to be found!

Scott comforted Amanda with assurances that he had to be somewhere close by. He advised he would be right over to help with the search. After hanging up the phone, Scott called Sally and Ken to help with the search. He then went to the backyard and called for Sieg.

Sieg, Melody and Kim were playing a game of "keep away" with the Frisbee but with Scott's command to come both dogs had run to his side. Kim saw the look of concern on Scott's face she asked, "What's wrong Scott?"

"Adam is missing, Amanda just called, someone broke the gate open. Adam is gone. I'm going to take Sieg and meet Ken and Sally. We are going to go look for him." Kim grabbed Melody's collar, "Melody and I want to help to." "Okay, pumpkin, you can help to. We'll take Sieg, his new tracking title may just come in handy, he can follow Adam's scent. Adam must be in the neighborhood somewhere."

Scott did not disclose his fears to Kim. He had not disclosed them to Amanda either. It was possible that Adam had been stolen. The broken gate was evidence that someone had wanted in the yard, probably for the wrong reasons.

Within minutes of Amanda's call Scott, Sally, Ken, Kim, Melody and Sieg arrived at her door. Amanda was relieved to see her calvary, she prayed they would help find Adam soon. Amanda was no fool, but just like Scott she was not willing to reveal her suspicions. How and why was the gate lock broken? Adam would not have left the yard without the gate being forced open. She smiled bravely at her search party. She would not allow herself to dwell on any other theories for now.

Sieg and Scott retrieved a blanket from Adam's bed and Scott allowed Sieg to take the scent. Sieg followed the scent all over the backyard and finally went out into the street. Everyone was sure he would lead them right to Adam. After only a few minutes Sieg stopped and stood confused in the street. The scent had been strong for only a short distance and then it seemed to vanish. Scott and Amanda continued to suspect the worst yet neither of them dared speak their fears.

The band of searchers divided up the neighborhood and walked for hours, calling for Adam. They talked with people in the neighborhood and searching the nearby park. No one had seen Adam.

Finally, Scott insisted that Amanda return home to rest. They could call the dog pound and the police and let them know of Adam's disappearance. Scott also called Dr. Stockman to alert him and other vets in the area in case Adam showed up injured at one of their clinics. All that could be done would be done and Amanda needed to guard her own health, now more than ever. Scott reminded her of his promise to Michael. He would not allow her to go on without rest, not while she carried a child.

Adam was young and strong and if there were any possible way for him to get back home he would. Again Scott and Amanda avoided their secret fear -- Adam had been stolen!

After the phone calls were made and Amanda had agreed to lay down to rest, Scott drove the others home. Later after he dropped off Kim and Melody and took Ken home, Scott confided his fears to Sally, "Sal, I hate to think the worst but I think Adam was stolen. The fact that Sieg could only follow his scent for a short distance seems to indicate that Adam must have been loaded into a car or something and driven away."

Sally confessed her own fears, "I've been thinking the same thing all evening but I didn't want to say anything to Amanda, she's just beside herself. What will she do if we can't find, Adam?" Scott signed, "I don't know. We better pray Adam comes home and Amanda doesn't have to go without him for long."

Chapter 7 -

The Search Continues

The jangle of the alarm brought Amanda straight up out of her bed. Morning was upon her, no time to waste as she hurried into her jeans and shirt. The sun would be up soon and the search would continue.

It had now been weeks since Adam had disappeared from the back yard. Again she chastised herself, "why, why didn't I take Adam with me? Amanda, you were so foolish to leave him alone in the yard unattended, even if it were for only thirty minutes." Adam had been, no, she corrected herself, "Adam is" a very outgoing, curious dog. He looked upon the whole world as a grand place to explore. He had been so content lying under the tree when she last saw him. A few minutes on his own would do him no harm. Adam would never have left his world in the backyard, He had always preferred the companionship of his mother and sister to exploring about. His only excursions had been to training classes, dog shows or car rides with Amanda and Michael. "Why?", She asked herself again. By this time she was fully dressed. She pulled her hair back into a ponytail and started down the stairs to the kitchen. Harmony rose from her mat next to the bed and followed. Amanda released Abby from her crate and opened the back door to allow the two dogs to make their morning rounds.

Amanda filled the water bowl with fresh water and prepared the dogs' breakfast. When she reached for the bowls she noticed Adam's empty dish. The tears fell. "Get a hold on yourself, Amanda Nelson, "Adam is coming home you must believe that."

Harmony scratched at the back door and Amanda busied herself feeding the two dogs. After the dogs finished their breakfast, Amanda picked up her coat and car keys. The jingle of the car keys brought the two dogs to attention. They raced to the garage door. Amanda opened the door and the dogs scrambled to the back of the station wagon. They waited for the door to be lowered. As the tailgate lowered, the two dogs jumped into the back of the wagon. Harmony and Abby, after all these weeks, knew the routine that was to follow. They did not know why they made these daily trips, but, like most dogs, they enjoyed the outing.

Amanda drove the neighborhood near her home. She stopped occasionally to check back yards in the area. She asked the morning joggers if they had seen Adam. She and Scott had posters made up weeks ago. The posters showed a photo of Adam and offered a reward for his return or for any information as to his whereabouts. By this time everyone in her immediate neighborhood and others throughout the town were familiar with her daily quest. Satisfied this morning that she had made a thorough search, Amanda drove to their next stop, the city animal shelter. Amanda checked with the clerk for any news of recent strays picked up in the area. She again searched the runs of the dogs already confined just in case the attendants just might have overlooked her beloved Adam. He had been gone for weeks and his physical condition may not be accurately represented on his photograph any longer. The attendants did know what a Boxer was, Tammy Henderson's reputation as the Boxer Rescue lady and her community education programs left little to the imagination. Tammy had educated them that boxers were not" fighting dogs." Still Tammy and Amanda had been faced with this issue the very first day Adam had disappeared. They had gone together to the animal shelter to alert them of Adam's disappearance. Upon showing a photo of Adam to a new attendant on duty he had exclaimed, "Oh, that's one of them pit bull fighting dogs, isn't it." Amanda and Tammy had been aghast at the remark, to think that Adam could be conceived as anything but the fun loving, warm, companion he had always been. They took the remark in stride, there were still people in animal shelters and pounds as well as some police officers and the general public still needing to be educated. Tammy, Amanda and other breeders in the area were still fighting hard to clarify the false assumptions concerning not only Boxers but any other breeds who just might fit the description of a "pit bull fighting dog."

Amanda, guided by Tammy's expertise, took the time that day to introduce Adam's mother and sister to the new attendant. As the weeks went by, all of the attendants at the shelter and all the police officers on every shift were either introduced or reintroduced to the Boxer.

Amanda and Tammy realized that most people are not malicious in their thinking just ignorant and uninformed about what a "pit bull or fighting dog" really meant. It was important that they understand fighting dogs were not a specific breed or breeds of dogs. Most of these dogs were bred and trained by despicable men who had no compassion for the animals they so brutally exploited. They knew too that they lived in an area where these practices were still present. They understood the authorities concern to protect the citizens of the town against a dog who truly was a menace to society. Caution should certainly be the first order of business when approaching any stray. They just wanted the officers and officials responsible for the picking up of these strays to also approach these animals with an open mind. Not a mind cluttered with misinformation or prejudice against any specific breed of dogs. Many dogs when approached by a stranger will offer some form of resistance. This resistance should not be always interpreted as aggression. Fear makes men and animals alike do stupid things.

Tammy herself closely watched for Adam, hoping at the very least he would come through her rescue program and she would have the delightful job of reuniting him with Amanda.

After the daily visit, Amanda was again satisfied that Adam was not at the animal shelter. She and the dogs drove to the local playground. It was Saturday and the children would be playing in the park. On weekdays Amanda and the dogs traveled to the schools in her area. Amanda had also educated the children and teachers about Boxers. Sieg's presence and Tammy Henderson's work in the community had helped Amanda's efforts in educating the children and the false label put on dogs of this type.

Amanda cautioned the children to still be very careful around stray dogs. They should always ask an adult for assistance as soon as possible when they encountered a stray at the playground. Amanda's Adam loved children and she wanted them to know that. She also wanted them to know that every dog was not as gentle as Adam. Children, Amanda observed were usually much more perceptive than many adults she encountered.

Several children spotted her station wagon as she parked near the park and hurried over to the car. Immediately the questions began, "Did you find him, has he come home?" The sad look on their faces always tugged a little harder on Amanda's already broken heart.

Although many children had never actually met Adam, his mother Harmony, his sister Abby and, of course, Sieg had made the children aware of the wonderful qualities possessed by the Boxer. Some of them had seen Sieg at the community events and when they learned Adam was Sieg's son they were even more concerned for his welfare. Each in their own way had done his or her part to help Amanda locate him. Some had helped with posters, some had walked their neighborhoods while others asked everyone they knew about seeing any stray dogs. Their efforts had not paid off yet. The children remained determined to help Amanda retrieve her "special fellow." Amanda spent approximately an hour with the children before loading the dogs back into the station wagon.

It was Saturday and she and the dogs would drive into the country side near the town and continue her methodical search for Adam. Someone had to know something about him, a dog like Adam does not simply vanish into thin air!

Harmony and Abby settled down in the back of the station wagon. Today was the long ride day they reasoned to themselves. On long ride days they would have the opportunity to see and meet new people along the way.

As Amanda turned onto the highway to head east, an old, dirty red pickup turned into the town from the east. The men in the pickup glanced at the woman with the two dogs in the back of her wagon then quickly sped away toward town.

Amanda recognized the pickup. She had seen it before in and about town. Like the other times, she paid little, if any attention. Her only thoughts right now were concentrating on Adam. She closely watched the roadway for signs of him or, God, forbid his body laying along the road. Amanda would not let herself believe the worst, that Adam was dead. No she would tell herself, she would know if that were true. Something kept driving her to make these searches week after week. She would not give up. Adam was out there somewhere and if he could, he would come to her. In the event Adam could not come to her, she would attempt anything to go to him.

Chapter 8 -

Hide & Seek

Adam awoke on his second day of freedom feeling better than he had in weeks. The nourishing meal the night before had eliminated the hunger pangs. The pain from the wounds on his body was beginning to subside. He stepped from the barrel where he had spent the night. He stretched and watched the sun rise from the direction he had traveled. His body shivered as he remembered the men. He should be off, he could not afford to stay in one spot too long. They would be searching for them. He took to the woods on the other side of the town. The trees would afford him some sort of camouflage from the eyes of those men searching for him.

He could keep the road in sight that led to the west. That direction seemed to continue to draw him. He saw nothing familiar to encourage him but he could not keep from traveling west. As he thought of his mistress Adam's gait increased. He had to hurry before the men could find him. She would protect him.

About mid-day Adam stopped near another farm to drink out of a pasture pond. He was not concerned about the cows standing about but he was ever watchful now for humans of any kind. Adam didn't know if he could trust anyone other than his mistress. The weeks of confinement and abuse confused him. The only human he wanted to see was his mistress.

His thirst satisfied, he rested in the woods just above the highway. There he could gaze down on the road and to the west. Adam was just about to begin his journey again when he saw the dirty pickup with the cages in the back drive slowly along the highway to the west. His fears were confirmed. The men were still looking for him. He was sure they could not see him from the road yet he stayed in his place until the pickup was long out of sight. A growl formed in his throat when the truck went by. Adam had learned fear at their hands. He had also learned anger, a deeper more volatile instinct than he or his mistress would ever have imagined him to possess.

Finally he began his journey again, always keeping himself out of sight of the vehicles traveling the highway. By the time the sun was ready to set, he had traveled a good distance to the west. Adam was hungry again. This time his fear of being discovered by the men in the pickup truck was much greater than his appetite. He would travel a while longer in the darkness. The cover of night would again be his friend. Somewhere out there was his mistress. That comforted Adam; the thought of the men being out there distressed him.

After a few more miles, Adam took shelter in the bushes. He circled to mat down the grass beneath his feet to make a soft bed. It was difficult for him to sleep in the complete open. Like his ancient ancestors Adam was a cave dweller. His crate had been his haven from harm at home. How he longed for the comfort his mistress and his canine companions would give him. There were times he had hated to be sent to his crate, afraid he would miss something. Those times seemed unimportant now as Adam lay listening to the sounds of the night. It was quiet except the wind rustling the leaves and the crickets chirping. It was not home but he felt safe for the time being. It was certainly a better place to sleep than the shed he been forced to sleep while enslaved by those men. Adam gradually relaxed and soon sleep was upon him.

He whimpered in his sleep. He dreamed of the days long behind him, the excitement of the show ring, the sights and sounds of the show site, the joy of being reunited with his mistress and the long days of fun and companionship with his mother and sister. These were the good dreams.

They were not the only dreams for Adam. The nightmares were beginning to fill his mind even when he slept. Adam awoke with a jerk, the man with the tobacco breath was just about to beat him! Adam was relieved to discover it was only a dream. There was no one in sight. Adam spent the rest of the night going in and out of a fitful sleep. He had been exhausted the first two nights of his freedom. Tonight the thoughts of the pickup truck and the men were again fresh in his mind. The fear of discovery would not let him rest.

Long before dawn, Adam was up on his feet and moving to the west. As the dawn broke, Adam approached another small town. It would be full light soon. Adam contemplated his choices of how to keep himself hidden from those he feared and hated. The town lay directly in the path of his westward journey. To the north were houses. Small businesses lined the main streets of the town and to the south was a small river.

Rather than risk being discovered in the town or near the houses, Adam chose to cross the highway. He traveled along the riverbank. There at least, there was some cover from the road. He could avoid the eyes of the humans in the town.

He made his way along the riverbank, taking time only to quench his thirst. As he rounded a turn in the bank of the river, Adam froze in his tracks. Just yards ahead of him sat a young man casting a fishing rod into the river. The man had not spotted Adam. He quickly took cover back behind the turn in the river bank. Now what would he do? The man blocked his path along the river. The sun was up and the town would soon be bustling with people.

Adam peeked around the riverbank; the young man sat in the same spot with his fishing rod in hand. He sang softly to himself with the fishing line well out in the river.

There was a distance of about 10' from where the young man sat on the riverbank and the actual edge of the river. Adam reasoned to himself. If he moved quickly and went undetected by the man until he was just a little further down the riverbank, he could certainly outrun him. It seemed the best choice.

Adam rounded the riverbank heading toward the man and hopefully to the riverbank beyond. Adam had only gone a few steps when the young man spotted him. The surprised look on the man's face quickly turned to a smile. Adam froze again and glanced at the man's face. Adam saw the smile. He stayed fixed in the same spot long enough to allow the man to speak.

"Well hello there, fellow, you're up and about pretty early aren't you?" The man had a soft voice. His smile was pleasant. Adam did not understand what he was saying but the way he was saying it allowed him to relax just a little. The man did not attempt to move in his direction. Adam stood his ground. They stood just watching each other.

The man took note of the dog's condition. He guessed he had been through quite an ordeal by the looks of him. "You look like you've missed a few meals, fellow. Somebody or something sure took a few bites out of you," the man said.

Adam began to feel less threatened by this man, but he was a long way from considering anything other than eye contact for now. Adam watched closely and jumped just a little as the man laid down his fishing pole. Adam was prepared to break and run. His fear was kept in check by the man's casual movements.

The man reached into a basket and pulled out a sack. "I don't have much to offer fellow, I think you could use these bologna sandwiches a lot more than me." He unwrapped the sandwiches and slowly tossed them in Adam's direction. Adam flinched as the man threw his arms out. The sandwiches landed near his feet. Adam was gathering his courage to bolt as the aroma of the bologna hit his nostrils. Adam gazed at the man again. What was the man going to do?

The man pointed to the sandwiches, "Go ahead, fellow, eat them up. I'll just go on home later and get me some more. My Mom won't mind when I tell her I fed them to a poor hungry dog. We both like dogs."

The aroma was tempting and Adam bent his head down to sniff the sandwich closest to him. His hunger pangs appeared in full force. Adam quickly devoured the first sandwich and then the second. The man still did not attempt to move toward Adam. Adam hesitated for a few moments and then started to make his way up the bank. Again the man did not attempt to move toward him.

"Looks like you've got someplace to be fellow. Hope the meal keeps you going for a few more miles. Somebody will be glad to see you."

Adam glanced back over his shoulder several times, continuing to put distance between himself and the man. The man had picked up his fishing rod started singing.

Adam proceeded along the riverbank and soon the man could no longer be seen. His voice, still singing softly, faded from Adam's ears. He had been the first human, other than the child in the wading pool, who had shown him any kindness. The food had been welcomed and Adams spirits were lifted a little. Maybe all the humans had not gone crazy after all.

It wasn't long until Adam left the town behind. He continued along the riverbank. He stopped only to rest and satisfy his thirst. The west still beckoned as the sun began to set on another day of freedom.

Chapter 9 -

Revelations

Amanda and the girls had covered many miles before the day ended; yet still no word on Adam from anyone. Sadly Amanda turned the station wagon in the direction of home, it would be dark soon and the night would block her view of the road and countryside. Tomorrow was Sunday, they would try again in the morning.

Long after Amanda returned home, played with the girls, fed them their dinner and settled in for the night she could not fall asleep. Adam was out there somewhere; her frustration flooded over her and she began to cry herself to sleep.

Harmony climbed on the bed and did her best to comfort her mistress licking the salty tears as they ran down Amanda's face. It was hard to deal with this, Amanda was now six months pregnant. She and Michael had planned so long for this baby. Now with Michael in Germany and Adam missing her entire world was coming apart. Their plans were for Amanda and the three Boxers to join Michael in Germany in just a few more weeks. How could she leave not knowing where or how her Adam was? Time was running out. She must find Adam and she must find him soon. She could not leave without knowing, it was unthinkable. Michael shared her devotion to the dogs, he would understand, wouldn't he?

Exhaustion won out and Amanda slept, her arms wrapped tight around Harmony. The sun was up when Amanda awoke the next morning. In her frustrated and exhausted state she had not set her alarm. Her body and mind had needed he extra hours rest. Amanda felt her unborn child moved within her. She realized she must begin to think of her child. Harmony stirred as she too, felt the baby's movement against her back. The comical look on her face gave Amanda a reason to smile, "it's my puppy, Harmony, you remember don't you?" Harmony cocked her ears at the word "puppy" and Amanda smiled again, "Come on girl, let's get started, we've got to find that wandering puppy of yours."

Amanda dressed, let the dogs out and fed them breakfast. Because the animal shelter was closed and the children would not be playing out quite so early this morning, she loaded Harmony and Abby into the station wagon and they started the day's search. The station wagon was backing out of the doorway when Scott pulled behind her, "Wait a minute Amanda, I've got something to tell you" he shouted. Amanda had not heard all he had said but she stopped the car to see what Scott wanted.

"Amanda, I have some news about Adam, or maybe what might have happened to him."

Amanda's heart leaped, "What is it you know, Scott, please tell me."

"Well, Amanda, I was down at the gas station near the end of the road yesterday afternoon and I heard some men talking about looking for a dog. They were talking about him maybe trying to get home."

Amanda listened still not quite comprehending what Scott was trying to tell her, "Go on, Scott, is there more?"

Scott continued, "It wasn't their dog they were looking for Amanda, I just know it." Amanda questioned Scott more, "What makes you think that, Scott, maybe you didn't hear everything they were saying."

Scott shook his head no, "Oh, believe me I heard it all, Amanda. They didn't know I was sitting around the corner when they put air in their tires. They said if they didn't find him soon they would just have to go out and steal themselves another fighter."

"Fighter, Oh my God," Amanda exclaimed. "Scott, what did these men look like? What kind of vehicle were they driving? Do you know who they were?

Scott stepped forward and put his arms around Amanda, "Take it easy Amanda, sit on the porch swing. I'll finish telling you what I know." "I've never seen them before, they don't live here in town. They were kind of dirty looking; one on them was a very big man. He chewed tobacco and he had a beard. They drive a dirty red pickup truck with a big cage in the back."

Amanda's heart took another leap, of course, the pickup truck, why she had just seen it again yesterday herself. She now remembered seeing it about town more than once. In fact, Amanda's memory flashed back, she had seen that same pickup truck the day Adam had disappeared. "Oh my God," she exclaimed again, those men stole my Adam. Scott, I'm going to the police to see if I can get some help in finding these men." Scott climbed in his own car, "I'll follow you there, Amanda, I can give them a good description of the men and a partial license number on the truck. When they did spot Sieg and me they jumped in their truck and took off, that's what really made me suspect they knew about Adam. When they looked at Sieg they did a double take. They looked like they were seeing something they recognized. If Sieg hadn't growled at them when they started to approach I think they would have talked to me. Instead they took off like I said."

Amanda was excited at first as she drove the few blocks to the police station. In that short time, however, she began to think of the horror of the ordeal Adam must have faced in the weeks gone by. All of her talks and lectures about the difference between her beloved Adam and the dogs used for fighting by evil men took an ironic turn. Adam may now be known as a "fighter" to these men and the circle of people they traveled in. Amanda would not allow herself to dwell on what could have happened to make Adam fight; he had always been such a gentle soul. "He's alive, and he did escape," she told herself, for now that was enough to deal with.

Amanda arrived at the police station with Scott right behind her. They leashed Harmony and Abby and went into the station's lobby.

Sgt. Blake was on duty at the desk. Amanda heaved a deep sigh of relief. Sgt. Blake was very familiar with the ordeal she had been going through and was very sympathetic. As he watched Amanda and Scott rush through the door he immediately came to the front of the desk, "Amanda, slow down before your hurt yourself, what's happened, what's going on?"

Amanda took a few minutes to catch her breath, "Its Adam, we've got some news about Adam."

Sgt. Blake circled the desk and offered Amanda a chair, "Sit and tell me about it." Amanda and Scott related to Sgt. Blake about the two men in the pickup.

Sgt. Blake cautioned, "Neither of you are sure that the dog the men were talking about was Adam, so don't get your hopes set to high."

Amanda tried to contain herself, "It is a start though, after all these weeks it's a start!"

Sgt. Blake went to the desk and took a pad and pen from the counter, "Scott, give me a description of the truck you saw, try to remember every little detail you can."

Scott began, "Well, it's red, a faded red, with dirt on the hood and sides, I remember that."

Sgt. Blake began to write on the pad, "Do you remember what make it was, was it a Ford or a Chevy or a Dodge?"

Scott answered, "it was a Ford, with a wire cage in the back, I remember reading Ford on the back of the truck as it took off."

Sgt. Blake kept writing, "Do you remember seeing any signs or emblems that stood out, perhaps a hood ornament?"

Scott added, "There was a dent in the drivers door and the license plates were out-of-state, the first three numbers were 666 followed by the letters STN. They also had a gun rack in the back with two or three rifles."

Sgt. Blake jotted down the license plate number, "that will be a big help. What about the men, Scott, can you describe them?" "Sure, said Scott, one of them was really big, about 6' or better and he looked like he weighed at least 250 pounds. He had a dirty black beard with a scar over his left eye shaped like a half-moon. The other guy was little, maybe 5' 6" and real skinny, his hair was a dirty brown and he had pock marks or something like that all over his face."

Sgt. Blake finished writing down Scott's descriptions, "Well this is definitely something to go on, I'll see that the different shifts are alerted to watch for this truck and the two guys in it. "If they show up in town again and are spotted, we'll make a routine traffic stop to see if we can gain anymore information about them."

Amanda realized it was not going to be a quick answer to her prayers; at least it was a beginning. Amanda inquired, "Will the cars also make a special watch for, Adam, just in case he is the dog who escaped from them, if Adam can come home I feel he'll try his best to get there."

Sgt. Blake agreed to alert the shift officers to the possibility of Adam showing up in town, "If he's spotted, we'll call you first thing, Amanda."

That was it, that was all Scott and Amanda could do at the police station for now. Amanda thanked Sgt. Blake for his understanding and as she and Scott walked to the door Sgt. Blake warned them both. "Amanda, Scott, we don't know for sure what kind of men we are dealing with here, don't you do anything foolish if you come across them yourself, you call us right away, promise?"

Amanda and Scott agreed they would call immediately if they spotted the truck or the men in town again. Amanda hoped that she did not have the opportunity to confront them on her own. She didn't know whether she feared them as much as she hated them and her emotions could very well cause her to do something very stupid if she did run across them.

This is one of those times she wished more than ever that Michael was home to help her keep her emotions in check. Michael was the level headed one where the dogs were concerned, well he was the level headed one in just about every case Amanda admitted to herself.

Almost as if Scott could read her mind, he reached out and took Amanda's hand, "You're really doing everything you can about this, Amanda, and don't worry we'll find Adam. Sieg and I will be available any time you need us." Amanda hugged Scott tight; this tall, kind hearted teenager was indeed a good friend and he was keeping his promise to Michael and Amanda loved him for it. She knew Scott was special. She fondly recalled the very first time she had spotted Scott and Sieg at their first dog show years ago. Scott had grown from a confused and angry boy into a fine young man of both strength and character.

Outside the police station, Amanda loaded the two dogs back into the station wagon. There was still plenty of daylight left and she told Scott she and the girls would travel back into the countryside on their search. Adam was out there somewhere. Hopefully he was the dog who had escaped from the men and was coming home to her. She wouldn't allow herself to think what would be happening to Adam if he were still in the hands of these men. Scott reminded her to be careful. He told her he would go get Ken and they would drive around town in hopes of seeing the pickup. Amanda turned the station wagon onto the highway headed to the East, that was the direction she knew she must travel and hopefully Adam was coming to her out of the west. If the dog who had escaped from those men was Adam she had to find him before those men did! Adam could not fall back into their hands. , She felt a knot form in her stomach. Amanda's heart ached for Adam.

Chapter 10 -

Refuge

*A*dam found himself at a point in the river by the end of the day where he had to again select the protection of the woods across the other side of the highway or to turn in the direction of the river. He waited for dark and then crossed the highway to the woods. The river was no longer going in the direction he wanted to travel. He took a last drink before he crossed the road and loped into the safety of the woods.

Adam found another spot in some bushes and prepared to rest for a few hours before continuing his journey. Off in the distance he could hear the howling of a dog, the soulful sound only served to remind Adam of his own loneliness. He thought about his mother and sister and remembered the nights by the fire as they all would cuddle together sharing the warmth of their bodies with one another.

Adam had been in the company of other canines since he had been gone from his home. These dogs shared only the instinct to survive with Adam, reduced to fighting for life itself. There had been no moments of warmth or happiness with the dogs he had encountered since he last saw his mother and sister. They were not dogs he wanted to remember. Even the bitches who had been brought to him for breeding had unwillingly accepted what the men forced them to do. Adam was an experienced stud but the unfamiliar surroundings and the circumstances of his imprisonment had made this once pleasant experience into an ordeal he had learned to dread. The first time they had brought a bitch to him, Adam was too frightened to perform. The men beat him when he had not bred the bitch. After that incident, Adam had done their bidding rather than take a beating. He had once enjoyed the company of a lovely lady now and then when his mistress had brought them to call. He had not enjoyed the experiences in terror the men had caused him.

Sleep was again fitful and Adam was on the trail again before dawn. By the middle of the day he faced another dilemma, the woods that had afforded him protection from the eyes of the humans traveling the road in their vehicles had ended. Ahead lay another open valley, sparsely dotted with a few trees and fields of crops. Most of the valley was open pasture and several farms dotted the rest of the landscape. He would not be able to travel completely out of sight.

Adam was determined to keep traveling west, he would just have to be cautious. His encounter with the young man yesterday had left him with no harm done. He would not seek out any human contact but he would at least consider that perhaps all men were not like his captors had been.

Running through the cornfields, he avoided contact with any humans at the first farm. By the end of the day he had made his way across about half the valley without encountering any real problems. A tractor had startled him once as he ran across a freshly plowed field. The human on board the tractor had paid no attention.

It was dark when he passed near another farmhouse. A dog's bark from the direction of the barn stopped Adam in his tracks. It was not a malicious bark, Adam knew that type of bark very well by now. This was more of a happy bark, a bark like he recalled making when he begged for his dish of food each night.

Food entered his mind and Adam figured, like with the Shepherd he had tricked, where there was a dog there may be food. He jumped behind an old pump house as the door of the barn swung open and a young girl came out of the barn. She walked to the house and entered the door at the top of the porch steps.

Adam could see light in the barn and in the distance he saw a Collie and her pups huddled in an open stall just inside the door. The Collie and her puppies were feasting on a large bowl of food. The saliva ran in Adam's mouth, he had not eaten since yesterday morning and the hunger pangs returned. Slowly he approached the doorway and stopped just outside, he could turn and run if necessary.

The Collie turned to see the strange dog standing in the doorway. She did not growl, she did not charge, she simply stood by her pups staring at Adam. Adam had seen that stare before, he remembered when his mother had puppies last year. He had wanted to see what was making the wonderful sounds coming from the box where his mother lay, that stare from his own mother was enough to warn him to stay back. His mother had kept him a bay for several weeks with that stare. Adam was wise in the ways of motherhood - don't mess with a Mama!

This Collie was not his Mama, but those puppies belonged to her and he would not attempt to go any further. The Collie would not have been much of a match for Adam after his "fighting experience" over the last few weeks but Adam's own faculty of understanding about puppies and mothers would not allow him to resort to the things he had been made to do. He would leave, he would not fight this bitch for her food.

As Adam turned to leave, one puppy spotted him and ran in Adam's direction. The Collie swiftly followed her runaway attempting to round him up before he reached the intruder. She was not quick enough. The puppy shot between Adam's legs, wiggling and yapping as only a puppy can. Adam dare not move, the Collie was fast approaching. He prepared to submit should she charge. Adam still did not want to fight her.

The Collie must have realized Adam's willingness to submit and when she saw he made no offer to harm her puppy, she relaxed her challenge.

Adam winced in pain as the puppy grabbed his jowls with his sharp puppy teeth. He still did not attempt to hurt the puppy. He trembled as the bitch began to sniff him. Adam could smell the food she had been eating on her breath, it reminded him of his hunger.

The Collie offered a friendly poke with her nose and Adam responded with a wag of his tail. The puppy had already lost interest as he ran back to the dish to finish his supper before his littermates had eaten it all.

Adam and the Collie stood together sniffing and poking at each other in fun. It had been a long time since Adam had felt like he could play with another dog.

The sound of the girl's voice brought him back to reality with a start, "Well, Bess, where did this gentleman friend come from?" Adam slunk to the ground in terror, she was much too close to escape back out the door.

The girl seemed almost as startled at his reaction, "Hey, take it easy fellow, I'm not going to hurt you."

Adam heard her voice, he didn't understand what she was saying but again like the young man the day before, she had a gentle sound to her voice. The girl sat on a nearby bale of hay and did not attempt to come in his direction. Adam stood his ground, not knowing what to do, the Collie seemed unconcerned about this human's intrusion and she went to the girl's side and climbed in her lap.

"Get down, Bess," the girl ordered, "I'm trying to make friends with your new fellow." Adam could have darted out the door at that instant but his instincts, although still somewhat clouded by his ordeal, left him no immediate reason to fear this young girl. The girl continued to talk softly to him.

Sarah thought to herself as she went over the dog with her eyes. He must have been through a terrible ordeal, but underneath the dried blood, mud and scars she could still see that this was a fine animal. Stray dogs had a way of showing up at the farm now and again. Sarah concluded from her quick observation this was not the average stray dog she had become accustomed to seeing in her twelve short years.

The dog looked terrified and ready to run at any minute so Sarah was ever so careful to keep her voice soft and soothing, "It's okay big guy, I won't hurt you."

Adam listened to the girl's voice, he was still very frightened but continued to sense she would not harm him.

The Collie and her pups banged their pan in the corner; they were through with their meal. The sound startled Adam. Before he could react, however, he was overwhelmed with Collie puppies all about him. They had all come to investigate the newcomer.

Adam did his best to keep his balance as the pups ran in and out his legs playfully pulling at whatever they could reach. Sarah stood up and called to the pups, "Puppies, come on."

At the sound of her voice the pups all followed Sarah back to the stall and Sarah quickly closed the door so they could not escape. Bess lay down in front of the door to wash herself after her evening meal. The pups busied themselves playing with one another.

Sarah walked back to the hay bale and sat back down, "That will take care of those little devils for now, they sure can be a handful."

Adam still stood his ground although the last few minutes he would have had the perfect opportunity to escape out the barn door into the night. The urge to leave was not as strong right now, the girl still offered no threat. The Collie and her pups seemed to trust her. Could he?

Sarah moved from the hay bale toward the door, "I'll be back fellow, I'm going to get you something to eat and a fresh drink of water, you stay here, okay?"

Adam understood only the word "stay" as he watched the girl walk from the barn to the house. He did not know what to expect. He allowed himself to sit, keeping watch in the direction the girl had gone. The Collie showed no signs of concern and continued her grooming.

Sarah ran into the house, "Mom, there's a dog in the barn and I'm going to feed it." Nancy Jacobs knew well her daughter's penchant for taking in stray dogs, she had seen quite a few come and go. Sarah had a good heart and oh how she loved the animals, "I'll give you some help, Sarah, wait while I get my jacket."

"No, Mama," Sarah exclaimed, "this one is scared to death and I'm afraid if you go with me he might run at the sight of two of us."

Nancy nodded in agreement, "Okay, Sarah, you're the animal expert, but if you need any help you be sure and call me."

Sarah promised as she ran out the door, "I will, Mama, just give me a little extra time with this one, he looks like he's been through an awful time."

Nancy watched out the back door as her daughter ran to the barn with the pan of food, she could barely see the strange brown dog in the light of the barn. It looked to be a good-sized animal and she wondered if Sarah were safe. Bess would have raised a fuss if the dog had been vicious, Sarah would be safe with her Bess there. Besides Sarah had a way with animals, almost a magical talent to sooth almost any of the animals she had managed to nurse back to health over the years.

Adam watched as the girl came back to the barn. She was carrying a pan. As she came closer he could smell the aroma of food. His mouth began to water, he had forgotten his hunger in the time he had spent in the barn.

Sarah stopped a few feet from Adam and placed the pan on the floor, "Here you go boy, this is for you." Adam watched as she again took her seat on the hay bale. The Collie rose to go in Adam's direction, "No Bess, that's for our guest, you've had your dinner."

The Collie turned and sat next to Sarah. Adam hesitated only a few seconds before beginning his meal. The food tasted good; he tried not to gulp it down too quickly but his hunger would not allow him to eat like a gentleman. Adam gobbled the food down with just a few bites - it was wonderful! This was the first meal he had eaten with any type of pleasure since he left his home. He licked his jowls and looked at the girl.

Sarah got up and walked over to some buckets sitting next to the stall, "I'll get you some fresh water, fellow. Just relax." Adam watched as she went to a water spigot and filled one bucket with water. Slowly Sarah carried the bucket to where she had placed the food dish and set it down next to the now empty bowl. This time she did not return to the hay bale but stood just a few feet from Adam.

Adam lapped up some water, his eyes kept watch of the girl. Just a few more laps and he was done, he did not want much water. The Collie came to his side and began to drink from the same bucket. Adam made no resistance he would gladly share the water with her. Adam continued to keep his eyes fixed on the girl. She sat now on the floor of the barn just an arm's length away.

The Collie walked to her and washed her face with her wet mouth, "Bess, cut that out, your getting me soaking wet."

Adam could recall his own mistress telling him to take his wet mouth away and it amused him to see the Collie play the same games he had so enjoyed with his mistress. The girl rolled on her side, laughing and trying to escape the Collie's licking tongue.

The girl continued to roll and suddenly she was directly under Adam's head right next to the water bucket. Adam gazed down into her face. She smiled and ever so gently caressed the side of his neck with her hand.

Adam did not back away though he was skeptical. The girl was close, her touch was gentle, even soothing and he soon found himself not trembling with fear but anticipation of another caress.

Sarah stroked his neck and reached to scratch behind his ear. Her hand settled just below the ear, a large gash had come dangerously close to tearing the ear. Sarah felt the tears begin to come in her eyes; this poor dog has suffered so much.

Adam cried out in pain as Sarah touched the gash. He backed away but did not attempt to retaliate.

Sarah spoke softly, "It's okay, fellow, I'm sorry I hurt you, I want to help you get better." The soothing voice worked; Adam allowed her to touch him again.

This time Sarah avoided touching any of the cuts and gashes. Sarah concluded from her brief examination, "You really need to see a vet, but it will take some doing to get you there I can see that."

Adam didn't know what the girl was saying. Exhaustion, his full stomach and the pleasure of her touch combined to work their spell on Adam and at last he lay down, his head coming to rest on the girl's lap.

Adam recognized love and for no other reason he entrusted his weary and beaten body to this girl with the soft voice and soothing touch.

Chapter 11 -

The Investigation

*A*manda and the dogs drove east the best part of the day stopping in each town to ask not only about Adam, but now to inquire if anyone had seen the pickup truck linked with Adam's disappearance. Her luck seemed to have run out for the day. No one she spoke with knew anything of her dog or the red pickup.

Somewhat let down, after such an enthusiastic start, Amanda and the girls returned to the house just before sundown. It was just a small let down, Amanda assured herself that she could follow through with this new information and with the help of the police Adam would come back to her.

There was a message on her answering machine from Sgt. Blake when she returned to the house. Amanda quickly dialed the police station. By this time Sgt. Blake had gone home for the day, but the officer on duty gave her his home phone number, Sgt. Blake wanted to talk with her as soon as possible.

Her hands shaking, Amanda dialed Sgt. Blake's number, what news did he have, did he know where Adam was? Amanda's mind raced as the phone rang once, then twice and then a third time. Maybe Sgt. Blake wasn't home. Before she could continue with that thought, Sgt. Blake answered the phone. Amanda almost shouted, "Sgt. Blake, It's Amanda Nelson, what have you found out?"

Sgt. Blake spoke in his typical composed voice, "Relax, Amanda, I don't have any bad news but just maybe a little good news."

Amanda collected herself immediately, "Okay, what were you able to find out?"

Sgt. Blake began, "I did some checking on the license plate and as you know we are close to the border and the license plates are from the next state over. The county they were issued from is only a hundred miles or so away."

Amanda tried to keep her calm, a hundred miles away, that's a long way for a dog lost and afraid.

Sgt. Blake continued, "I contacted the police department and sheriff's office in that area to see if I could learn anything about these men and any dog fighting activities in their state. As you know there is a law against such fighting in our state but their state does not yet prosecute dog fighters. They have legislation being processed right now but until it's a law they can't do much about these guys. He told me there were some dog fighters active in the area and there were rumors that they were stealing dogs to bring to their fights. The pickup truck was listed to a couple of fellows they suspected were involved in these activities. The sheriff told me he would put out a bulletin to see if they could contact the men and do some checking on his own. He's a dog lover Amanda and he took this thing personal just like me. I think if there's anyway he can help us he will. He's going to call me back tomorrow and get more information from me on Adam. That's really why I called. You mentioned that you had a tattoo on the inside one of Adam's legs. I'd like to have that number to give him along with the photo I'm going to Fax to him tomorrow."

Amanda was encouraged, "Yes, he does have a tattoo on his left rear leg, on the upper side of his inner thigh. It's his AKC registration number, wait a minute and I'll get it." Amanda ran to her desk and pulled out the drawer where she kept the files on the dogs.

She should know his number by heart but she was too excited to think straight. She found Adam's file, pulled out his AKC certificate and raced back to the phone, "Sgt. Blake, his number is WF-436706."

Sgt. Blake repeated the number, "WF-436706, okay that will do it for now Amanda, get some rest I'll talk to you again tomorrow." Amanda hung up the phone and placed Adam's registration certification back in his file. Also inside the file was the copy of his championship certificate from AKC, his pedigree and several photos. Adam was indeed a handsome dog. A photo of Adam and Sieg together and another photo of Adam caught her eye. He had been eight weeks old. She could not hold back the tears and again they fell.

Adam was only three years old but it seemed like a lifetime that he had shared her life. Harmony and Abby were special to her as well but Adam was her pride and joy. Adam was a strong, active example of his breed and his potential as a stud dog was endless for not only did Adam possess the fine physical characteristics of his father but it seemed in the few litters he had so far produced his puppies also exhibited the fine qualities of their sire and grand sire. It would be a shame if Adam could not continue to help the breed. Amanda stopped herself short again, she would not allow herself to think of the negative things that had or were happening to Adam. Adam was on his way home and that thought was the only one she would concentrate on for now.

Amanda began her nightly routine and after dinner she wrote a letter to Michael telling him the latest news about Adam's disappearance. It was well after midnight when she went to bed. As she drifted off to sleep she smiled as she remembered the photo of Adam as a puppy, "What a cute little guy," she murmured.

The next morning was Monday and although the search routine remained pretty much the same, Amanda did not drive into the country to extend the search. Instead she drove the girls back to the house, locked them safely in their crates inside the house and proceeded to her doctor for her checkup. She had decided as she returned from the doctors she would stop by the police station to talk with Sgt. Blake.

Amanda drove the few blocks to the doctor's office. Dr. Mac was one of a dying breed, a small town doctor who still made house calls when needed and even delivered babies. The high cost of malpractice insurance has just about driven his kind out of business. Amanda was thankful that Dr. Mac had remained.

Dr. Mac was to her like Dr. Stockman was to her Boxers, not only their physician but a good friend as well. Amanda had been raised in this town and when she and Michael had decided to buy a house the small town atmosphere had attracted them both. Dr. Mac was just an added bonus.

As Amanda entered the waiting area of his office, he popped his head out the door, "Hello, Amanda, come on back I'll be with you in a minute." There was no need to ask what room, Dr. Mac only had one examining room. Amanda walked back the hall. Julie, Dr. Mac's nurse, followed behind her with her stethoscope wrapped around her neck, "I'll weigh you in and get your blood pressure, Amanda."

Amanda sat as Julie performed her tasks and noted the results on her chart, "How's it doing, Julie?"

Julie answered, "It's pretty good, Amanda, but you look awfully tired, better be prepared for a lecture from you know who?" "Exactly who would that be," Dr. Mac questioned as he walked into the room?

Julie mumbled something to herself, gave Amanda a wink and said, "Your on your own, honey."

Amanda smiled, "Thank's a lot."

Dr. Mac read Amanda's chart, "Your doing okay, Amanda but by the looks of you your not getting enough rest; you look worn out. I know you are obsessed with getting that darn dog of yours back. Amanda you have to start thinking more of yourself and your baby."

Amanda nodded, "Please don't scold me, I've got some wonderful news, we may finally have a lead on Adam."

Dr. Mac was pleased at the enthusiasm in Amanda's voice, "Well you don't say, did someone find him, come on girl tell me the scoop, your just busting to, I can tell."

Amanda explained all about Scott spotting the truck and the men and Sgt. Blake's help.

Dr. Mac cautioned, "Just be sure you don't do anything foolish young lady, you let the police handle this."

Amanda answered his order, "Doc, you know I'll be careful but I intend to do everything I can to help get Adam back and that's that."

Dr. Mac gazed at her face, "Amanda I know you too well, I wish Michael were here to take you in hand."

Amanda grinned, "You know very well when my mind's made up no one can change it. Not even Michael."

Dr. Mac had to agree, "that's true enough. You sure have cornered the market on the word stubborn. You go find that darn dog and be quick about it. Maybe then you'll concentrate on having that baby you're carrying about."

Amanda slid down off the examining table and gave him a hug, "Don't worry, Doc, this baby is very important to me and I wouldn't risk its life for anything, but Adam is important to me too. I'll see you in two weeks and I'll bring Adam with me, you just wait and see."

Dr. Mac smiled, "Okay you do that and get some sleep between now and then."

Amanda nodded her agreement as she went out the door of the examining room. She was out the door and in the car like a flash; she was off to the police station to talk with Sgt. Blake.

As Amanda pulled in the drive of the station she saw the police tow truck go by. It was towing a dirty, red, Ford pickup. Amanda's heart raced, "My God, they've caught them!"

Chapter 12 -

A Time to Mend

Sarah sat with the big dog's head in her lap, caressing his head. She spoke to him in her soft tones. Slowly he relaxed and began to wag his tail each time she spoke to him. Sarah spoke, "You look like you've had some pretty good fights. You sure don't look like the type to go around picking fights."

Adam wagged his tail again, he didn't know what the girl was saying but she sounded sincere. Sarah finally stood up and Adam came to a sitting position, "Now what," he wondered?

Sarah turned to the Collie, "Bess, I'm going to put you in with your babes for the night and I'm going to let the big guy sleep in the barn."

The Collie trotted over to the stall where her pups had been confined and waited for Sarah to open the door.

Adam could see the puppies all huddled in a ball, sleeping peacefully as the girl opened the stall door. The Collie trotted in and quickly made herself a bed near the puppies.

Sarah closed the door and walked to the stall next door; it was also empty. Because the weather was mild this time of year the horses spent the nights out of doors. She pulled a blanket from the door of the stall and laid it in the straw of the stall, "Come here boy, this can be your bed for the night."

Adam didn't know what to think of this, the blanket looked inviting and he certainly was tired. He didn't like the idea of having the door of the stall close on him, he would feel trapped again. Adam felt he could trust this girl; he just wasn't sure, he trembled a little.

Sarah noticed his trembling, "It's okay fellow, I won't close the door, and come on I'll spend the night with you." Sarah walked in and lay down on the blanket. She then coaxed the dog to come in the stall with her.

Adam walked very cautiously into the other stall. A few more minutes of the girl's tender touch and soft voice and he lay down at her side. It was good to feel the closeness of a human friend again.

Sarah rested with the dog until she was sure he was in a deep sleep. Adam was exhausted and he slept peacefully for the first time since leaving home. Sarah quietly crept out of the stall and ran to the house. She would tell her mother she was going to spend the night in the barn with the latest "stray" and she also wanted to talk to her father. She should warn him about the new dog in the barn in case he or her brother, Joe, might come barging in tomorrow morning and scare the poor dog even more.

Tim Jacobs sat at his desk in the small den just off the kitchen mulling over the latest batch of bills.

Sarah ran in and gave him a hug, "Hi, Daddy, I heard you and Joe drive in a little while ago but I couldn't come to greet you." Tim gave his daughter a knowing smile, "I know, Pumpkin, your Mama told me you've got another stray in the barn. Well what is it this time?"

Sarah answered his question quickly, "I think it's a Boxer but I'm not sure. He looks something like the picture of the Boxer I remember seeing in my dog book."

"A Boxer?", Her father pondered, "I wonder what a Boxer is doing in these parts? They usually don't use them for farm work." Sarah agreed, "It sure doesn't make sense to me either, but he's really pretty scared and he's been in some terrible fights by the look of him. Can we have the vet look at him tomorrow when he comes to check the horses, Bess and her puppies?"

Tim agreed, "I guess so, Honey, but are you sure he'll let the vet get close enough to him to treat him?"

"I'll do my best to keep him from being too scared," Sarah answered. She gave her father a quick hug and ran upstairs to her room. She quickly grabbed her pillow and another blanket. She also snatched the dog book lying on her dresser.

As she went out the back door Sarah gave her mother a hug, "I'll see you in the morning, Mama."

Sarah returned to the big dog's side in the stall. Adam stirred only slightly as she crawled in beside him on the blanket. He was snoring loudly; a good sign that he was indeed in a deep sleep.

Sarah and Adam awoke to the sounds of the puppies yapping loudly in the next stall and Bess's deep bark. Bess was tired of being with her little ones and it was time to be rescued from their harassment.

Adam had been comfortable snuggled next to Sarah and as he began to realize it was not his mistress and he was not in his own bed he again began to tremble.

Sarah reached down and stroked his head, "It's okay fellow, you're still safe with me."

The sound of Sarah's voice again soothed Adam's fear. He followed Sarah as she went to the stall door to rescue Bess from her puppies.

Bess was out of the stall in a flash, leaping and wiggling with joy at the sight of Sarah. Adam was soon caught up in her enthusiasm and bounced at Bess's side.

Sarah quickly closed the stall door halting the escape of one puppy, "Wait a minute you little guys, I'll let you free in a few minutes but for now your Mom needs a rest." Sarah walked to the barn door and headed for the house. It was time to feed not only the animals but herself.

Adam followed her to the door but stopped before walking outside into the sunlight. Bess continued, following closely at Sarah's heels.

Sarah stopped when she saw Adam's reluctance to leave the barn, "Come on fellow, it's okay, I'm just going to get the feed pans for your breakfast."

Adam cautiously stepped into the open area just outside the door. Sarah encouraged him further by bending to her knees and calling softly to him.

Once he reached Sarah's side, he trotted along side Bess; he was not completely comfortable in being in the open but was relaxed with their company. Sarah reached the back door, opened it and walked in side.

Bess sat smartly on the porch with Adam standing at her side. Adam could smell bacon cooking and although he was not starved like he had been lately the smell did awake his appetite. He could hear other voices inside and the sound of the men's voices made him shiver with anticipation. Would these men come after him? Surely they would not, the girl would not have led him and the Collie into a trap? Adam did not know much about this girl other than she had been kind to him and the Collie adored her. He would be all right.

Sarah emerged from the back door with two pans of food and placed them on the porch. One pan she placed in front of Bess, the other pan she placed in front of Adam. She returned to the house and came out with yet another large pan, "You both stay here and eat your breakfast while I take care of the little ones."

Adam had begun to eat his food when he realized the girl was headed back to the barn. He began to follow. The girl turned, "No, fellow, you stay here and eat your breakfast in peace, the little ones will be all over you soon enough."

Adam wanted to return to the barn with her. He glanced over at the Collie and she was busy eating. Maybe it would be okay, she seemed comfortable enough staying behind.

Sarah continued to the barn and opened the stall door to release the puppies from their confinement. Like their mother, they were excited to see her, darting under and through her legs, jumping at the pan she held above their heads. Sarah placed the pan of food down outside the stall and the puppies pounced on the pan like little savages who had not eaten in weeks. Sarah noted to herself, it would soon be time to start teaching these little ones some table manners.

As the puppies devoured their food, Sarah busied herself cleaning the stall where they had been confined, raking up the straw and puppy droppings into a pile and shoveling them onto the wheelbarrow that sat nearby.

She was putting fresh straw in the stall when Adam appeared at the door. He had finished his food and ran straight for the barn. It was not going to let this girl out of his sight for any length of time. Bess followed closely behind.

As Adam walked through the door he was overwhelmed by the mass of puppies charging in his direction. Like the night before, he stood perfectly still. He remembered his mother's litter and realized that these puppies were just that, puppies. They were no threat to him, just a little annoying.

Bess began to chase about and soon she and the puppies rushed out of the barn and back toward the house.

Sarah laughed as Adam tried to navigate the thundering herd as they passed by, "They sure have lots of energy, don't they." Adam turned to watch them race toward the house. He shrank back as he saw a man standing on the porch.

Sarah was at his side now, "That's my, Daddy, fellow, you'll be okay, he won't hurt you."

The man troubled Adam as he approached the barn. Sarah bent down and held his neck as though she was protecting him, "Steady fellow."

The man stopped a few feet from them, "So, Pumpkin, this is the new boarder on the Jacobs spread. He's sure a big one."

The man spoke with a soft voice, not harsh and loud like the men Adam had escaped from. Adam relaxed just a little.

The man made no effort to come any closer, he stood back the same distance, "Hello, big guy. What's a dandy dog like you doing in these parts?"

Adam's tail wagged, the man made no effort to reach for him. Like Sarah the night before Tim walked to a bale of hay close to the entrance of the barn and sat.

Sarah coaxed Adam in the direction of the man, "come on fellow."

Adam did not distrust the man, he seemed friendly but he had been wrong before when those awful men had come to his yard. They had acted friendly at first; however, once they had him, locked in that cage in the back of their truck they turned into two ugly fellows.

Adam stood his ground, observing this man for several minutes and then every so cautiously he began to approach. Just a couple feet away, Adam stopped again and watched for signs that the man may be preparing to lunge.

Tim made no movement, sitting perfectly still and as Adam looked into his face he smiled and the man spoke softly, "Easy, fellow. No one is going to hurt you."

Adam liked his voice and stepped just a little closer; he could smell the man's scent and the scent from his clothing, animal scents mixed with the mans.

Adam stretched his head forward and nuzzled the man's hand resting on his leg. Adam trembled, waiting for what he didn't know, just half expecting this man to react like the "animals" he had been forced by to obey their commands.

The man continued to speak softly, "Take your time fellow, you should like what you smell."

Sarah approached her father and the dog and sat next to her father on the bale of hay. Adam moved past the man to Sarah and sat almost between them.

Ever so slowly the man's hand raised and he placed it under Adam's nose. As Adam sniffed the hand, Sarah reached over and patted him every so gently on the back of his neck. The tension disappeared and Adam began to relax; this man could earn his trust too. The three of them sat for several minutes, Sarah and her father talking to Adam and with each stroke of Sarah's hand Adam relaxed even more. Finally, Adam allowed the man to stroke him.

Sarah then stood up, "I'm going to do my chores now, Daddy, I think we can coax this guy to cooperate when the vet gets here." As Sarah walked back to the barn, Adam lingered for only a moment at the man's side before following the girl. He clearly knew who he wanted to be with as he trotted along side Sarah and the Collie as they entered the barn.

Tim Jacobs smiled and shook his head, that Sarah and her strays, how they all loved his gentle daughter.

Sarah gathered grain in a wheelbarrow and wheeled it through the doorway and down a small path at the side of the barn that led to the horse pasture. The Collie and Adam followed close at her heels while Sarah's father gathered up the pups and put them in a small fenced area next to the barn, a puppy playpen. They were to young to be underfoot when the horses came in for their feed.

Just over the hill from the barn lay the pasture. As the trio, two dogs and Sarah, approached the gate Adam heard the ground begin to pound and looked in the direction of the sound.

Six horses raced in their direction, three mares with foals at their side raced for the feed rack located just inside the gate. Adam trembled at the size of these animals thundering in their direction. He glanced at the Collie who seemed unconcerned about this development. They were safely behind the gate Adam began to reason to himself; the girl had always had good control of the situations he had encountered up to this point so he was willing to give her some more of his trust.

The horses stopped at the gate and began milling around the feed rack. Sarah opened the gate and wheeled the wheelbarrow over to the feed rack.

The horses, completely familiar with the routine, took their places at their proper racks and waited for the grain to be poured. Adam stood watching these giants eat their grain in contentment. The foals particularly intrigued him. They were much bigger than Adam but he could sense they were babies.

Adam had followed along with the Collie inside the gate and had stood with her at a respectful distance from the mares while they had received their grain. Now with the mares busy eating their grain Adam's curiosity continued to build over the little ones.

One foal, a little speckled Appaloosa filly, was also curious. Almost simultaneously, Adam and the filly began to approach each other to inspect what they both figured was a very strange creature indeed.

As the filly reached her nose out to nuzzle at Adam and he stretched his own muzzle in her direction, Adam did not see the mare turn her head and begin to charge. He was too involved with the little filly, gazing into her big brown eyes to realize he was in danger.

Bess, however, knew full well what was coming and seconds before the mare reached Adam she sprang at the mare, turning the mare away from Adam. Adam heard only the thunder of the mare's hooves and saw only the blur of the Collie's coat as she jumped into the air.

The filly turned and ran, kicking up her heels as if this were a grand game while Bess placed herself between the mare and Adam. Adam then realized what Bess had done as he saw the mare snorting in defiance.

Sarah had been busy playing with another foal when she saw what was happening. She made her way to the mare's side and gently took her halter, "Easy, Velvet, he won't hurt your little one." The girl's soothing voice again worked it's magic as she turned the mare around and led her back to the feed rack.

"Good girl, Bess," Sarah praised the Collie. Adam wagged his tail in agreement, this Bess was a real handy dog to have around and had certainly gained Adam's respect.

The horses fed, Sarah wheeled the wheelbarrow back to the barn. As she and the two dogs came back outside the barn a pickup truck pulled into the barn yard. Adam cringed at the site of a pickup and slunk back inside the barn. Sarah watched him, he stood just inside the doorway watching the truck.

Sarah knew the pickup belonged to Dr. Hager, the vet. Apparently this vehicle or a vehicle like it made this dog uneasy. Sarah called Bess back to her side. Bess had run on ahead to greet Dr. Hager; there was no question that she liked him. "Come, Bess," Sarah called and the Collie reluctantly, yet obediently returned to Sarah's side. Sarah placed Bess next to Adam, "You stay here with our guest, he needs a little courage right now." Bess sat at Adam's side and whined just a little as Sarah walked to the truck. Adam remained motionless, watching and waiting. He felt somewhat safer with the Collie at his side; he was just not sure of this new arrival.

Tim Jacobs walked from the farmhouse and greeted Dr. Hager, "Hi, Cal, thanks for coming out, I've got a pretty good day's work lined out for you."

Dr. Hager glanced in the direction of the two dogs, "I see, Sarah, has herself another stray."

Sarah smiled, "Yep, wait until you see this one, he's a dandy, I think he's a Boxer." Dr. Hager again glanced at the new dog, "Your right, Sarah, that's a Boxer, wonder what he's doing in these parts?"

Sarah agreed, "That's what Daddy and I would like to know. He's had a rough time of it and I think he'll need some attention from you today."

Dr. Hager raised his eyebrows, "I hope this isn't going to be a wild one like the bobcat kitten you had me fix up a few months back."

Sarah laughed, "Oh, he's not wild, just scared but I think I'll be able to coax him into letting you patch him up."

Dr. Hager opened the back of the pickup and as the tailgate slammed down Adam darted back into the barn. Sarah's father helped him unload his equipment and Sarah walked back to the barn.

She found Adam hiding in the safety of the puppy stall. Sarah reasoned that it was the pickup truck that truly frightened this dog and she went to his side to reassure him. Adam continued to tremble and relaxed only after Sarah had stroked and patted him for quite awhile.

Once Adam was reasonably relaxed she called the Collie back to his side, "Bess, you stay here with him while I fetch Dr. Hager."

Adam was reassured by the Collie's presence and sat at her side. He watched the girl leave the barn. He felt safe in the barn and had no intention of venturing out to that pickup truck.

Sarah found her father and Dr. Hager in the puppy pen. Dr. Hager was just finishing giving an inoculation to the last puppy in Bess's litter. "That takes care of the little ones, Sarah, now I'll get to Bess and your new friend. Where did he get to anyway?" Sarah pointed in the direction of the barn, "He took off inside when you slammed the tailgate of your truck. I don't think he's as much afraid of you as he is that truck. Do you suppose he just doesn't like pickup trucks?"

Dr. Hager closed his bag, "Could be, Sarah, he might have had a bad experience in one of them, dogs are funny that way. Sometimes they can remember unusual things." Sarah, her father and Dr. Hager walked into the barn.

Adam saw them approaching, he was not completely terrified after all the girl was with them. He did trust her completely. Adam also felt the Collie would be his ally. He was sure of that too after the incident with the horses earlier.

Sarah entered the stall while the two men waited outside. Adam wagged his tail as she approached. Sarah sat next to him and wrapped her arms around his neck and gently pushed Adam in a sit position. She coaxed Bess to lay beside her, "Okay, Daddy, you and Dr. Hager start in but take it slow and easy."

Adam felt secure with the girl's arms around him. The sight of the men approaching frightened him more than just a little. Trust, he must trust this girl and his instincts to break away and run gave way to the instincts he had been raised with, trust and love.

Dr. Hager laid his bag down and gently nudged his hand in Adam's direction.

Adam jerked back just a little but a reassuring word from Sarah, "Easy," and he sniffed the man's hand. He could smell the puppy scent on the hand. Surely he would do Adam no harm or Bess would not have let him near her little ones.

As Dr. Hager began to pet and stroke him, Adam felt the gentleness in his big hands. Dr. Hager shook his head, "He's got some really nasty bites and tears. The rip on his ear is really bad too. I'm afraid I'm going to have to put him under to do any good. There's just too much work to be done with local anesthetic."

Tim volunteered, "I'll clean off the table in the summer kitchen, you can operate in there. It's clean and there is plenty of light."

Dr. Hager agreed, "Okay, I'll go ahead and give him the shot now. We'll carry him to the kitchen. I don't want him to fight the anesthetic; he's pretty calm right now." Dr. Hager filled his syringe and administered the shot to Adam.

Adam winced when the needle broke the skin but the pain was nothing like the beatings he had received. Adam began to feel sleepy, slowly his eyes closed as he listened to the girl's soothing voice, "Good boy, you're going to be just fine."

Dr. Hager worked quickly, stitching and mending the big dog with expert precision. Once the wounds were cleansed and stitched he examined the dog further, checking his mouth, he determined that he had a broken canine and several teeth were chipped. The teeth would have to be repaired but not today. He did not want to keep the big dog under anesthetic any longer than necessary.

Dr. Hager's adept hands continued to examine the big dog. He was a very good example of his breed. His physical condition overall was impressive, considering his shallow sides and loss of some muscle tone. Dr. Hager raised the dog's back legs to exam his groin area. As he raised the right leg, a tattoo on the dog's upper left thigh caught his eye, "Well, look what we've got here, this dog has a tattoo."

Sarah glanced down at the numbers and read them aloud, "WF-436706, that sounds like an AKC number to me."

Chapter - 13

Questions & Answers

*A*manda couldn't get out of the car fast enough. Her stomach, swollen with her unborn child, made it difficult to slide in and out from behind the steering wheel with any great ease. Hurrying made it even more difficult. She struggled to her feet and walked quickly to the station door.

Sgt. Davidson was on duty at the desk. He recognized Amanda and shouted, "Hey, did you see what's outside, looks like we might have the dog fighters in custody. I'll call Sgt. Blake, he's in one of the interrogation rooms. He's listening to the detectives question the suspects."

Amanda nodded, "Please, is there any sign of Adam?"

Sgt. Davidson shook his head, "No, Amanda, they didn't have any dogs with them. They were caught attempting to steal a dog from a yard just a couple blocks from you."

Amanda sat on the bench near the desk and waited for Sgt. Blake to appear. As she waited Scott and Sieg appeared from the rest room. Sieg bounded across the room to give Amanda his usual greeting. "Scott, what are you doing here? Did you hear the news?"

Scott grinned, "Oh I heard the news all right, Sieg and I helped with the arrest." Amanda waited for Scott to tell his story of the mens capture.

Scott began, "Well Sieg and I were out walking the neighborhood doing our usual patrol for the pickup when I spotted it. The truck was parked just down the street in front of the Clawson's' house. You know the Clawsons? They have a pair of Staffordshire Terriers. When I spotted the truck we went to the Kelly's house and I asked them to call the police. Sieg and I stood guard until the police arrived. While we were waiting, the men got out of the truck and headed for the Clawson's' backyard. Sieg and I watched them climb over the fence and before they could come back over the police had arrived. They were sure surprised to see the police when they came back over the fence. I think they were even more surprised when they saw Sieg standing there. It was just like that day at the garage when they saw him. They both looked like they were seeing a ghost. Sieg took one look at them and it was all I could do to keep him back. He's never reacted so aggressively to anyone before. I only hope we can find out where they might be keeping Adam."

Scott finished his story just as Amanda saw Sgt. Blake walking down the hall. He took her hand and helped her to her feet, "Come with me Amanda, I want you to hear what's going on back in the interrogation room."

Amanda followed Sgt. Blake into a small room where they could observe Detective Hanson and two men on the other side of a partition. It was obvious the men did not know they were being observed from the hidden surveillance room.

Sgt. Blake offered Amanda a chair. "Sit down, Amanda. Let's hear what they have to say. Detective Hanson is one of our best, he'll get to the bottom of this."

Amanda sat staring at the men remembering the descriptions Scott had given a few days before. There was the large man with the dark, scraggly beard and the half-moon scar on his forehead. The other man was indeed smaller, skinny, with greasy brown hair and pock marks all over his face. Not a handsome pair of humans. Amanda trembled to think that these people might have held the fate of her Adam in their hands.

During the questioning Detective Hanson verified that the two men had been in the area before. The big man spoke. "Just because we've been here before doesn't mean we're criminals. We weren't doing nothin wrong. We were just in the yard looking for a dog we lost."

Detective Hanson questioned, "Why would you be looking for your dog in a fenced back yard with a locked gate?"

The big man shrugged his shoulders, "There's no tellin where that dog gets to. He's always jumpin in and out of fenced yards. Detective Hanson continued his questioning. He tactfully managed to get the men to admit just a little more by allowing the two men to observe a police bulletin concerning dog fighting activities.

This time the small man revealed. "We don't fight dogs in your state, we just buy dogs to use at home."

The big man scowled at the smaller one. "Keep you mouth shut, Marvin, you don't need to tell them nothin about dog fightin." "Who said anything about dog fighting?" Detective Hanson asked.

The big man just scowled at the smaller man, "Marvin, don't you say another word." At this point Detective Hanson excused himself. He told the men he was going to make a phone call and he left the interrogation room. Sgt. Blake and Amanda remained in the surveillance room where they could still see and hear the two men. Detective Hanson joined them. After some discussion, they agreed to separate the two men and perhaps get more information out of the smaller man called Marvin. Marvin seemed ready to spill all he knew but the larger man known as Jake was far too intimidating.

As the officers observed the two men from the surveillance room it was obvious by his stony stare that Jake was in charge. Neither man spoke but the cold stare coming from the Jake's eyes confirmed his control over Marvin. Jake Homestead obviously controlled people and animals with fear and hatred as his tools for many years.

Jake threatened. "You best keep you mouth shut, Marvin, or I'm going to kick the hell out of you when they cut us loose." Sgt. Blake and Detective Hanson returned to the room and Sgt. Blake escorted Jake out of the room. Jake was not happy about the separation. He exited the room cursing and ranting to Marvin, "Remember what I said, Marvin."

Amanda watched and listened as Detective Hanson began to question Marvin Homestead. With his professional skill and savvy Detective Hanson was able to get Marvin to begin to answer his questions. Marvin admitted that they had been looking for stray dogs. He also admitted they came to this area a lot to look for "strays." Marvin insisted that it was Jake's idea to come here to look for strays. They did some dog fighting and they would take the strays home. Marvin insisted he had nothing to do with the dog fighting. He just helped Jake round up strays. It was obvious from Marvin's voice that Jake did intimidate him.

Amanda sat on the edge of her seat as Detective Hanson pushed a photo in front of the Marvin. The photo was the one of Adam that Amanda had furnished the police department.

Detective Hanson watched Marvin's face. "Have you seen a dog like this before?"

Marvin glanced at the photo. "Yep, that there's a pit bull, a real fighter. He's like the one where we got picked up, Yep, we had us one just . . . " Marvin stopped in mid sentence.

Amanda held her breath. She was sure he was going to say something about Adam.

Detective Hanson continued. "Did you have a dog like this?" Marvin squirmed in his seat, struggling to keep from volunteering any information yet he seemed ready to tell all just to be done with this persistent detective. A long silent pause. Amanda moved even closer to the viewing screen.

Finally Marvin answered. "Yep, we had us a dog just like that but we don't got him anymore. He ran away a week or so ago, probably laying dead in the woods somewhere."

Amanda's heart sank. No her Adam was not dead. She would not believe that. From the look on Marvin's face, she felt he didn't believe it either.

Detective Hanson asked, "Where did you pick this stray up, Marvin?" He wanted Marvin to think he believed his story about only picking up strays in the area.

Marvin volunteered. "We found him wandering around here. He sure was friendly until old Jake threw him into the back of our truck. By the time we got him home and starved him a couple days he wasn't quite so tough. He did real good his first fight but Jake had to beat him a bit. He sure was a fighter."

Tears formed in Amanda's eyes. Her poor Adam, what terrible things these men must have done to him to make him fight so. Amanda softly cried to herself as she listened to Marvin go on about their dog fights.

Sgt. Blake, Scott and Sieg entered the surveillance room. Sgt. Blake observed Amanda's tears and led her from the room. "You've seen enough, Amanda," he said. "We'll get all the information we can. I'll call you later. It may be a cold trail but at least now we have a trail to follow."

Amanda walked back out into the afternoon sunshine., the tears still glistening in her eyes. Scott and Sieg walked beside her to the car. This time there were no words from Scott; he couldn't find the words to comfort her.

Sieg instead offered his own form of consoling as only he could. When Amanda sat in her car Sieg nuzzled her softly with his velvet muzzle and placed his paw in her hand. His eyes glanced at her face and he licked away her tears. In his own way he was saying, "It will be all right, Amanda, our Adam is okay." Amanda hugged Sieg and buried her face in his neck and cried.

Scott offered to drive her home and Sieg laid on the seat beside her with his head now in her lap.

As they drove home, in silence, Amanda stroked Sieg's head. Thoughts of her years with Sieg and Adam traveled through her mind.

Adam had been a wonder from the day he was born. A typical Boxer he had loved to tease her and please her. His championship title had been easy.

Like his father, Adam had easily finished his championship. Adam had been just short of his second birthday. His awards included two five-point majors at the biggest shows in the country. Since then he and Amanda had gained one of his AKC obedience titles. They had been busy working toward his second when he had been stolen.

Amanda recalled too Adam's gentle nature. He had never been aggressive and always got along well with other dogs and animals. Thoughts of her Adam tearing the flesh of another dog were frightening. The thought of Adam's flesh being torn by another dog was even worse. That thought initiated another flow of tears.

Amanda attempted to hearten herself. Adam had escaped. That they knew for sure. Adam was out there somewhere, searching for her and his way home. Marvin was wrong. Adam was not dead.

Tomorrow she would again begin her search. She and the girls would find him! Somewhere someone must have seen him. Adam, like Sieg, was a people dog. No matter the horrors Adam may have endured, Amanda, believed with all her heart he would find a friend. Adam could always find and make a friend.

The drive home was complete. Scott helped Amanda into the house. From there he telephoned Ken to give him a lift back to the police station to pick up his car.

After Scott and Sieg had gone, Amanda put the girls out in the back yard to exercise. The thoughts of those dreadful men having been in the area today made her shutter. Thank God she had kept the two girls indoors when she left for her appointment with Dr. Mac that morning. Later Amanda packed a small suitcase in preparation for her journey. The girls would travel with her. She prepared their travel bag too, putting in leads, water dishes, food dishes, food, water and her doggie first aid kit. Amanda prepared for several days on the road. She was not coming home until Adam was found!

Chapter 14 -

Adam's Dilemma

*A*dam woke from his sleep. He found himself lying in the stall on the blanket he and Sarah had shared the night before. He felt strange. His wounds did not hurt as much as they had before his nap. He raised his head to look for Sarah. He could not see her, but he could hear her gentle laugh. Slowly Adam staggered to his feet and feebly walked in the direction of the laughter.

Adam arrived at the door to see Sarah playing with the puppies in the barnyard. Bess lay a short distance away under the tree. The two men Adam remembered in his dream were busy doing something with the large mare who had charged Adam in the pasture. Adam felt his balance going. He laid down just inside the door watching the activities. He wondered why he was so weak.

Sarah spotted him first and quickly corralled the puppies back into the pen. She didn't want them descending on the poor dog in his present condition. Bess helped her; She skillfully herded her offspring into the pen. Sarah walked over to the stray.

Adam wagged his tail. He licked the Sarah's face as she bent down to pet him. "Well, fellow, you've had a good sleep and you should feel lots better in a few more days." Sarah walked to the puppy stall in the barn and returned with a bowl of fresh water. Adam drank the cool water and again gave the girl a grateful lick. Sarah coaxed the big dog back to the stall with the blanket, "Come on fellow, you still need lots of rest. You'll be safe here." Once Adam was comfortable she encouraged Bess to join him, "Come on, Bess, lay down with him for awhile and maybe he'll be content to stay put." Bess curled up next to Adam and began to wash his face. Adam relaxed and then laid back down to rest. He remembered the wonderful baths his mother had given him as a puppy. He drifted off to sleep again dreaming of his gentle mother.

The rays of the sun the next morning brought Adam awake. He had slept peacefully the rest of the day before and all night too. Bess and the girl were gone. His ears heard the commotion of the puppies and feed pans rattling. He poked his head out the stall door and saw the girl bustling about.

She turned to his stall with a pan in her hand. "Well, good morning sleepy head, how about some breakfast?"

Adam was hungry. He had slept through dinner last night. He quickly ate the pan of food placed in front of him. Bess stood a short distance away eating her own breakfast. With his own breakfast gone, Adam approached Bess. She willingly allowed him to help her finish her breakfast. Sarah smiled at the pair. It was good that they were not going to argue over food. Dr. Hager and her father had decided that the Boxer must have been used in dogfights. He might be a little vicious if provoked. Sarah had agreed to be careful with this dog but her heart told her she really had nothing to fear. The sight of the two dogs sharing the dish of food convinced her. Bess and her puppies were safe too.

Adam followed the girl all morning as she did her chores. He was getting the routine around this place down pretty good. At lunch time he followed Sarah and Bess to the back door of the house. There he had been introduced to Sarah's brother and mother. Although still very cautious around these two new people, Adam was beginning to gain confidence in his new surroundings. The girl and her human friends had done nothing to harm him. Adam had not greeted them with the irresistible Boxer attitude but had not greeted them with fear or contempt either. Unlike the two men who had held him a prisoner for so long, these were good people. Sarah he trusted completely. She would not allow them to harm him. Adam was sure of that. Sarah was a friend, he could always find a friend.

As the days came and went, Adam healed from his wounds. A good bath washed the stink and dirt from his body. His coat began to glow with a healthy looking shine. Sarah made him feel wonderful, he adored her. Adam was confused. He would like to stay with Sarah and her Bess. However, there was still a strong force calling him to his mistress and the home he had known all of his life. He would have to go on sometime the instinct to find home was strong. For now Adam would be content to heal and bask in the warmth of the sun and Sarah's love.

Adam could not know that Sarah and her family were trying very hard to get him back to the home he so longed for. Dr. Hager had taken the AKC number tattooed on Adam's thigh and had begun to trace the registration with the organizations in the area who kept records of tattooed dogs. Dr. Hager said it may take several days to come up with anything but he would do his best to find out where the dog belonged.

Sarah's father decided he would report the dog to the local sheriff. The next time he saw Matt Richards in town he would check to see if anyone had reported a dog like this Boxer stolen. Both Dr. Hager and Sarah's father agreed that this dog was a valuable and well bred animal. Somewhere, someone must be waiting for some good news. It may take time to find them.

For now Sarah enjoyed the Boxer in her life. He was a wonderful dog, handsome and intelligent. Obviously someone had taken sometime to train him. He quickly responded to her commands to sit, down and come. This was not an ordinary dog by any stretch of her imagination. Sarah tried to suppress her feelings but as each day passed she found herself becoming more attached to this dog. A small part of her secretly and selfishly wished he would be allowed to stay with her and Bess. It was not an unusual wish for a girl with a heart the size of Sarah. She was always trying to keep her heart from ruling her head in such matters. Sarah's heart, her head came to realize, was a tough one to rule. Little did she know that Adam was having the same problem. Stay or go, what would he do? Neither Sarah nor Adam knew what lay ahead.

Chapter 15 -

Amanda's Journey

Early the next morning Amanda packed up the station wagon, preparing to leave. Just as she turned the girls out in the back yard for some final exercise the phone rang. It was Scott. He was calling to check on her. Amanda told him of her plans. Scott was very concerned for her safety, but his objections could not change Amanda's mind, she was determined to search for Adam. Sgt. Blake had called both Scott and Amanda earlier that morning advising them he had to release the Homesteads from custody. With no witnesses or physical evidence to prove they had actually stolen Adam, the police could not charge them with theft. Marvin Homestead's testimony had given them plenty of information but not the evidence needed to prosecute. A citation for trespassing on the Clawson's' property, a traffic citation for an expired inspection sticker and faulty brake lights were the only charges the police could pursue. The Homesteads paid their fines and were released.

Scott reminded Amanda of Sgt. Blake's warning to be careful if she planned on searching for Adam. There was no doubt the Homesteads would continue to search for him too. If they could dispose of Adam there would be no evidence to prosecute them for theft.

Sgt. Blake had urged Scott and Amanda to just call the police if they spotted the Homesteads again. Amanda remained adamant. She was going on this search. The best Scott could do was to make Amanda promise that when she arrived in the town where the Homesteads lived she would contact the sheriff immediately. There were no laws against dog fighting in the next state but stealing was still against the law. The theft of an animal such as Adam would be considered a felony no matter from where he had been stolen

Amanda was disappointed that the Homesteads had been set free. She was more anxious than ever to get a start. God, help us if they found Adam first! She told Scott she would call with any news and hung up the phone.

Scott laid the phone back in its cradle and turned to Sieg. "I don't know Sieg, Amanda may be getting in over her head. I hope she talks to Michael about this."

Sieg cocked his head; he didn't know what was causing the look of fear in Scott's eyes. Sieg stood alert, prepared to stand guard.

Amanda placed the phone number and address of the sheriff in the packet of photos of Adam. She was going to distribute the photos as she traveled along. She quickly loaded the girls in the car, glanced at the map and backed the car out of the drive. She could not hear the phone ringing as she turned the corner and headed for the highway.

Amanda drove all morning, stopping only for gas and to exercise the girls and her. Being pregnant, Amanda could not drive as long a distance without having to stop. The little one was playing havoc with her bladder these days. She did not want to push herself to the point of exhaustion. She had promised everyone she would take care of herself. When she had called Michael last night to tell him of the latest developments he had not wanted her to go. He insisted that she allow the police to handle the matter. An argument ensued. Somewhat begrudgingly Michael finally had agreed to let her make this journey but only if she promised to be gone just a few days. The moving date was fast approaching and Amanda would need lots of rest before her journey to Germany. Amanda had agreed with her head, however, her heart said she was not leaving without Adam.

Amanda drove through the small farming communities toward her destination. The countryside was familiar for the first seventy-five miles. She had driven this road before in her quest for Adam.

By mid morning she was in new territory. The towns became smaller and father apart. So much territory for a dog such as Adam to disappear. Amanda's heart strings were tugged with the feeling of desolation Adam must be feeling so far from home. She slowed the car as she made a turn in the road. A short distance ahead a pickup and horse trailer were about to enter the highway. The sign on the side of the truck read, "Jacob's Appaloosa."

Amanda strained to see into the trailer. She loved horses and hoped to catch a peek at the trailer's cargo. She was rewarded for her effort. Inside the trailer she saw a lovely Appaloosa mare with a young foal at her side. She drove past the trailer and soon left it behind.

Shortly after one o'clock Amanda and the girls arrived in the small town where they would begin their search. Amanda stopped at the gas station on the outskirts of the town and inquired about the location of the sheriff's office.

The attendant at the small garage supplied her with the information she requested. She also received some news she had not expected. While putting fuel in the car, the attendant observed the two Boxers in the back of the wagon. "Hey, I've seen that kind of dog around here before."

His surprising remark immediately brought Amanda to his side. "Where did you see one like this and when?"

The attendant, taken back by Amanda's excitement hesitated for a moment. "Well, I chased a dog like that way from my garage a week or so ago. He stole my Shepherd's food and managed to get the darn dog all tangled up in his chain."

Amanda questioned further. "Are you sure it was this kind of dog? Have you seen him since? Was he hurt or bleeding?

The attendant stepped back, "Hey, lady, slow down, I can only answer one question at a time." Slowly the attendant gave Amanda the information she had asked for. Yes, he was sure that dog was one of those Boxers. No he had not seen him since that evening he chased him off. By the looks of the dog he chased off he'd been in some pretty good fights.

Amanda was cheered as she got back in the car and drove to the sheriff's office. At least Adam had made it into town. He had also used his head to get his food. The fact that he had outsmarted the Shepherd indicated he was still a very capable dog. With a good meal he could have gotten further on down the road.

Amanda arrived at the sheriff's office and introduced herself to the deputy on duty. The deputy escorted Amanda to the sheriff's office. Amanda and the sheriff introduced themselves. Sheriff Richards was warm and friendly. He assured Amanda that he and Sgt. Blake would work together and try to get Adam back. Getting some hard evidence on the Homesteads was also one of their goals.

Sheriff Richards took some posters of Adam. He advised Amanda he would have his deputy post them throughout the county. When Amanda told him that the gas station attendant had spotted Adam nearby, Sheriff Richards was encouraged. They walked back into the entry way where he proceeded to post one of Adam's posters on the bulletin board. Amanda sat on the bench near the water cooler. Sheriff Richards gallantly offered her a drink and Amanda gratefully drank the cool water.

Just as Amanda took the last swallow of her drink, a woman and small child came through the door. They walked passed Amanda to the deputy's desk. It was obvious that the woman and child were the deputy's wife and daughter. The child ran forward yelling, "Daddy, Daddy, we brought you your lunch."

Amanda smiled, remembering the child she carried. She thought of Michael's delight at having a little girl or boy to call him Daddy.

The woman glanced in Amanda's direction then her eyes rested on the bulletin board above Amanda's head. "What's that sheriff, is that a poster on a mad dog or something?"

Sheriff Richards answered. "No, Kelley, the dog belongs to this lady here. We have some dog fighters in the area and we think they took him from her yard several weeks ago."

The woman moved closer to the poster. "You know, Tom, I think I've seen that dog before. "Beth come over here a minute."

The little girl climbed down off her father's lap and came to her mother's side.

Amanda's heart took another leap as she waited to hear what else the woman had to say.

"Beth, the mother asked, do you remember the doggie I chased away from your swimming pool a couple weeks ago?"

The little girl answered. "Un huh, he was a really nice doggie, Mommy but you chased him away."

The mother explained, "I thought he was one of those pit bull fighters. He was standing just inches from my Beth. I shot over his head just to scare him off. I'm sure that's the kind of dog he was."

Amanda felt the blood rush to her head. "You shot at him. Did you hit him?"

The woman backed up some as she saw the look on Amanda's face, "I didn't hit him, I told you I just shot over his head to scare him. I didn't know who's dog he was. I was just protecting my child."

Amanda realized she had frightened the woman, "I'm sorry, you didn't know. My Adam is such a gentle soul. He dearly loves children."

The woman relaxed. "I wish I would have known that. I would have tried to catch him for you if I'd known."

Amanda nodded her head. "I know, you had to put your child's safety first."

Sheriff Richards added to the conversation. "Kelley and Jeff live a few miles to the East of town. He must have come from their place through town. At least he was headed in the right direction if he was trying to get back home."

Amanda agreed. "He's heading west toward home." That means I might have passed him on the way here today. I'll have to start traveling back west. Adam is somewhere between here and my home."

Sheriff Richards cautioned. "You just be careful and take your time. If you run into Marvin and Jake Homestead don't you dare attempt to deal with them on your own. You get to a telephone and call me."

Amanda agreed. "I wouldn't attempt any kind of contact with that pair unless I see Adam with them. I just don't know what I would do then."

Sheriff Richards warned her again. "Just use your head young lady. We want to get enough evidence on these two to prosecute them. They've been operating in this area for a long time and we want to put a stop to it. This is the best opportunity we have had so far." Sheriff Richardson escorted Amanda back to the station wagon. "There's a small motel about twenty miles back west. Why don't you check in there for the night? Get some rest and start in the morning? I'll call you there if I hear anything." Amanda drove back the twenty miles to the hotel. She scrutinized the roadway for any signs of her Adam. She doubted very seriously if he would be in plain sight but her heart wanted him to be there.

Amanda arrived in the next little town and found the motel that Sheriff Richards had recommended. She stopped at the office to inquire if they would allow dogs in her room. The lady in the office peered out the window to look at Amanda's dogs. She questioned, "There pretty big dogs, you going to let them run loose in your room?" Amanda answered, "I'll crate them after their exercise. I'll keep them on leads when they are out of the room. They are both extremely well behaved. I assure you."

The clerk handed Amanda a registration form. "Just make sure they don't get loose and I guess it will be okay."

Amanda quickly filled out the registration and obtained the key from the clerk. She drove to the end of the building where her room was located. She opened the door, unloaded her luggage and then took both dogs out of the car on their leads. She walked them around for several minutes before taking them into the room with her. The room was more than adequate and clean, it was a good place to rest and take a nap. Amanda remembered her promise to Michael and Dr. Mac, she and the girls curled up on the bed and soon they were all asleep.

It was nearly 7:00 PM when the phone rang. Amanda was awake immediately. It was Sheriff Richards. He had no more news to report but wanted to make sure she had arrived at the motel okay. Sheriff Richards also wanted to warn her that the two men, Marvin and Jake, had been seen in town later that afternoon. Sgt.

Blake had called the Sheriff to advise they had been released from custody. Obviously they had headed straight home.

Amanda felt uneasy about that news. She was determined she would find Adam before those men had a chance to harm him again. She thanked Sheriff Richards for the warning and hung up the phone. She thought about calling home to her answering machine to check for messages. She decided instead to get something to eat first. She had eaten a good breakfast before they left home that morning but had only eaten an apple and some cheese for lunch. Amanda was eating for two now and the baby needed a meal. She unloaded the dog crates from the back of the station wagon and placed them in the room. There was a small restaurant just across the road from the motel. She would walk over there and get some dinner. She put the girls in their crates and gave them their dinner. They could eat and relax until she returned. She would exercise them again.

Amanda sat in the corner of the restaurant facing the front window. From there she could keep her car and the motel room in sight. She was concerned. The two dog stealers were back in the area somewhere. She was just finishing her bowl of soup when young man carrying a fishing pole walked from behind the motel. He headed for the café, strolling across the highway. He put his fishing pole and pail down just outside the door. He entered the café. As he passed Amanda he shot her a big grin, tipped his hat and gave Amanda a big, "Howdy." His smile was contagious.

Although Amanda was usually leery of strange men she instantly took a liking to the young man.

He walked on by and sat at the counter, "Come on, Maggie, I need a glass of milk and a hamburger. I'm not going to catch my supper today it looks like. The fish just aren't biting."

The waitress answered, "Your Mama said you'd be coming. She is going to the quilting circle at the church this evening. Said you might be hungry when you showed up. She only gave you three sandwiches for your lunch today."

The young man smiled. "I know, just not enough for a growing boy. Sometimes I have friends come to call while I'm fishing so I do share my lunch from time to time."

The boy and the waitress were still visiting back and forth as Amanda finished her meal. She brought her ticket to the cash register and the young man flashed her another grin as she turned to leave. Amanda again returned the smile.

She walked across the road back to the motel. She opened the door to her room and brought the girls out for their last exercise of the day. While standing there with the girls, Amanda realized she hadn't left a poster at the café about Adam. She walked to her car and retrieved one of her flyers. She walked back across the highway with the girls. It would only take a few minutes to post the flyer. As Amanda approached the girl at the counter to ask permission to post the flyer, the young fisherman was paying his ticket. "I can't help admiring your dogs, Miss. You know, I saw one just like them a few days back, gave him one of my sandwiches."

Amanda's heart took yet another leap. Quickly she handed the young man one of her posters. "Is this the dog you saw?"

The young man took the poster from her hands and studied the photo. "I'm pretty sure that dog looked like this one. He'd been in a terrible fight it looked like but I'd say this was the same dog. He was sure glad to have one of my sandwiches. He seemed friendly but he was awfully afraid."

Amanda felt her knees shake. She sat on a stool. Her Adam was still alive. He was still making his way in the direction of home. "Oh, Adam," she thought to herself, "hang in there fellow. Please get him home, God," she prayed.

Both the young man and the waitress searched her face for a sign of what she needed to help. Finally Amanda gained her composure, "That's my dog too. He was stolen from my back yard several weeks ago by dog fighters in this area. He apparently escaped from them. He seems headed home. At least he's traveling in the right direction so far."

The young man spoke with concern. "Those dog fighters must be Jake and Marvin Homestead. They're a couple of mean characters all right. I hope you dog doesn't get tangled up with them again before he gets home."

Amanda stayed and talked to the young man for sometime. When she left the café, he walked with her back to the motel. He cautioned Amanda again as he started to leave. "Keep and eye out for those two men and call Sheriff Richards if you spot them. I sure hope you get your dog back.

Amanda mustered another smile, "Thank you, I'm sorry I didn't get your name."

The young man beamed another one of his captivating smiles. "My name's Hank, Hank Barlow. Pleased to meet you Miss."

Amanda answered. "Amanda, call me Amanda. Thank you Hank for the kindness you showed to Adam. When he's back safe at home I'll bring him by to see you sometime. He's really a great dog. I know Adam would like to thank you himself."

Amanda watched as Hank crossed the road and disappeared down the road toward the town. There were some good people in this world too. Hopefully Adam would find some more friends like Hank as he traveled toward home.

Amanda placed a short overseas call to Michael before going to bed for the night. Michael was enthusiastic about her journey and the clues she had discovered. He too cautioned her not to get involved with the Homestead boys. Amanda assured Michael, just as she had Sgt. Blake and Sheriff Richards. "I'll be very careful, Michael. I promise I won't do anything foolish but I'll never let those men get their hands on Adam again if I can stop them."

Michael recognized the conviction in Amanda's voice and knew Amanda was adamant about continuing the quest. "Just be careful, Honey. I love Adam too but I love you and our baby more. Let's hope we all can be together soon."

Amanda bid Michael good night and curled up on the bed with Harmony and Abby. Tomorrow they would continue their journey. Amanda was convinced that Adam was somewhere between here and home.

While Amanda slept Michael telephoned Scott. He advised Scott of Amanda's whereabouts and the latest developments. With

Scott's parents permission Scott and Sieg would travel the next day to help Amanda continue her search. Amanda may need their help. Michael would feel better if Scott could provide his and Sieg's protection. Why was Amanda so bullheaded?

Chapter 16 -

Sarah's Quandary

*S*arah hung up the phone. "There isn't any answer, Daddy, we'll just have to try later. I left a message on the answering machine, I just hope the darn thing works."

Tim Jacobs watched his daughter's face. "You know, Pumpkin, when we get in touch with this dog's owner he'll be leaving." Sarah nodded; she had hoped she had hidden her feelings. "I know, Daddy, he belongs with his rightful owners. But, I'm sure attached to him."

"I know, Pumpkin, but you know how tough things are sometimes. It's just like when we sell off the calves and the foals from our spring crop. Sooner or later we have to part with just about everything and everyone in our lives."

Sarah agreed. "I know, I know, I'll just try to call again later." She walked to the back door. There she found Bess and the Adam laying on the back steps waiting for her return. She sat beside them both on the step. She patted Adam's head. "Look's like no ones at home at your house."

Adam cocked his head to the side as she spoke. He wasn't sure what she was saying but he knew she was talking to him. He began to wag his tail with all his might.

Sarah reached out and hugged his neck. "I sure hope whoever is missing you will be glad to see you. I'm not going to like seeing you go. That's for sure. Come on, let's go feed the horses." Sarah and the two dogs trotted off on their normal routine. At least for now the Boxer was all hers.

Later that evening Sarah tried the phone number Dr. Hager had given her again. With still no answer. Sarah left another message on the answering machine. She wondered where these people could be so late at night. Didn't they care about their dog? She began to hope they just didn't want him anymore and were ignoring her message. If they didn't call back maybe she could convince her Dad to let the Boxer stay.

The next morning the entire place was busy. Sarah's parents and her brother, Joe, were heading for a horse sale at the county fair. Normally Sarah would have enjoyed the thoughts of an outing but she really didn't want to go this time. She begged her parents to let her stay home. "I'll be fine here. The dogs will protect me and I know where the shotgun is if I need it. What if the people who own the Boxer call and there's no one home?"

Tim Jacobs didn't like the idea of leaving Sarah at home alone. He also knew it was important to get in touch with the people who owned the Boxer. "I tell you what, Pumpkin, you can stay home this morning but right after lunch I'll be back to get you. If you haven't heard from the dog's owners by then chances are you're not going to today. Besides there's no need for you to miss the entire fair."

Sarah agreed to the arrangement. She watched as the pickup and horse trailer drove out of sight. She tried the phone number another time, still no answer. This time she left no message on the answering machine. She had given them one last chance and now it was up to the owners to call her. If they didn't want their dog back, Sarah would give him a home. He had already taken ownership of her heart. She walked outside the house and gathered the puppies up into the puppy pen. It was a beautiful day, just perfect for a long walk. Sarah, Adam and Bess, strolled off over the meadow toward the woods. Sarah's patience had run out. She would not sit around on such a beautiful day waiting for the phone to ring. If the dog's owners did call then they would have to wait until someone got home.

Sarah was angry. She did not know these people but she did love this dog. To ignore him was unforgivable. Sarah's temper was her biggest weakness. It often led her to trouble. Today would be no exception.

Chapter 17 -

The Trail Grows Warmer

$\mathcal{A}$manda woke at the first light of dawn. She did not want to miss a minute of day light. She dressed and exercised the dogs. She walked to the café for her own breakfast. She left the girls in their crates eating their breakfasts. A glass of orange juice, some cereal and two eggs were plenty. Amanda visited with the waitress while she ate.

As Amanda walked back to the motel a sheriff's car drove up. It was Sheriff Richards. Amanda related to him what she had learned from Hank the night before. She explained she was going to continue her way back to the west in hopes that she might come across someone else who knew about Adam, or better yet Adam himself.

Sheriff Richards advised Amanda he would drive to the next town ahead of her and talk with the local people there. He took some of Amanda's posters. They agreed to meet at Noon in the town where they could compare notes. In the event he was called on an emergency Amanda could call his office. Sheriff Richards would give any information he might have to the dispatcher to relay to her.

Amanda loaded the crates and the girls into the back of the station wagon and walked to the office to pay her bill. Before driving off she thought about calling home to see if there were any messages on the machine. It was possible that someone by now had seen Adam's posters in this area and would have called her number at home. She obtained some change from the desk clerk and used the pay phone just outside the lobby. Amanda dialed the code for her answering machine. She waited for the phone to ring. The answering machine began to play. "Hello, my name is Sarah Jacobs, I live in Granger County. I think we may have a Boxer that belongs to you. The tattoo on his leg is registered to you. Please call us at 918-555-3030." Before Amanda could catch her breath, another message began. "This is Sarah Jacobs again. I think we have your Boxer. Please call us at 918-555-3030."

Amanda scribbled the number on the back of her motel bill. Her hands were shaking so badly she could hardly write the number. She walked back into the motel lobby and asked for more change. "Do you know anyone by the name of Jacobs?" She asked the clerk.

The clerk shook his head, "No, what county do they live in?". Amanda tried to remember the name of the county on the message. "Ah, Granger, it was Granger County." The clerk still shook his head.

"Well this is Granger County all right but they might live further west, sorry I don't recognize the name."

Amanda thanked the clerk and raced back to the pay phone. She dialed the number. Her heart was pounding in her ears as the phone rang, and rang, and rang. No answer, there was no one home. Amanda thought of Sheriff Richards, perhaps he would know a family named Jacobs. She would drive to the next town where they had decided to meet at Noon. Amanda left the phone, got in her car and spun her wheels and loose gravel as she pulled out onto the highway. A few miles down the highway she calmed herself. Driving like a crazy person was not safe for her, the baby or her dogs. Adam was safe. She knew that now. It was up to her to keep herself from harms way.

Harmony and Abby settled down in their crates as Amanda slowed to a reasonable speed. Whatever had gotten into their mistress?

It was nearly forty miles to the next town and Amanda drove the distance at a safe speed. She stopped only once at a small gas station to fuel her car and to exercise the dogs. A cold drink of water for the dogs and a cold Diet Coke for her and they were back on the road. It was only 10:00 am when she drove into the town. She was early for her Noon meeting with Sheriff Richards. She would use the time to call the phone number again. She also could ask around town to see if anyone knew the Jacobs. She was confident and reassured. Today Adam would be back home where he belonged. Amanda did not see the dirty red pickup truck with the Homestead boys inside. They traveled through the town toward the west. Amanda walked into the small grocery store as the truck drove past her.

Fortunately, the men did not spot her station wagon with the two Boxers in the back either. Had they spotted them they may have tried to try steal them. Instead they headed to the countryside to find some "fighting dog bait" for their latest acquisition. In the cage in the back of their truck was a large Rottweiler they had stolen the night before. Fighting bait was small kittens, puppies and other small animals they used to give the dogs they fought the killing instinct. They had seen a sign along the highway near the Jacobs place, "Collie Pups For Sale." They had also seen Tim and his family headed for the County Fair. It would be a good day to snatch some pups.

Amanda asked the grocery clerk at the front of the store if she knew a family named Jacobs? The clerk did not know. She called the store manager over. "Ben knows everyone in these parts, if they live near here he'll know them."

Ben Ford answered the call from the clerk.
Amanda introduced herself and then asked, "Do you know a family by the name of Jacobs?"

Ben Ford smiled as he answered. "I sure do, their boy, Joe is dating my granddaughter. They have a small farm about ten miles east of here. Are you looking for an Appaloosa or some Angus cattle?"

Amanda's mind flashed back to yesterday's drive. Hadn't she passed a trailer with an Appaloosa mare and foal inside? Of course, she remembered the pickup and long horse trailer. She also remembered the big mailbox and the sign on the side of their truck, "Jacob's Appaloosa," she said out loud.

Ben started to give her directions but before he could say another word Amanda ran from the store and headed for her car.

Ben called after her. "Hey, don't you want directions to the Jacobs place?"

Amanda answered him. "No, I remembered where it is, I passed it yesterday?" Amanda remembered her scheduled meeting with Sheriff Richards. "Would you do me another favor, Ben?"

"Sure little lady," Ben agreed.

"Would you please tell Sheriff Richards when he shows up in town at Noon to meet me at the Jacobs place. Tell him they have my dog and he's safe." Amanda shouted out the window as she drove by, " Thanks for your help."

Amanda drove east back in the direction of the Jacobs ranch. She left Ben Ford standing out in front of the grocery store scratching his head in confusion.

In just a few minutes Amanda knew she would have Adam back. The long ordeal would be over. Amanda would have been wise to wait for Sheriff Richards. Her wisdom, however, had been replaced with the tug of her heartstrings. Like Sarah, Amanda's emotions would lead her to a disturbing predicament before the day was done.

Chapter 18 -

The Rescue?

$\mathcal{S}$cott and Sieg had started out early the next morning. They traveled to meet with Sheriff Richards in the Homestead boy's hometown. By now Amanda should have checked in with the sheriff and maybe he could tell Scott Amanda's whereabouts.

Scott watched the countryside as he drove looking for any signs of Amanda, Adam or the Homestead boys. Like Amanda, Scott had not given up hope that Adam was alive. He only hoped they were not too late in this rescue attempt.

Scott stopped for gas shortly around 10:00 AM. As he finished pumping gas he observed a sheriff's car across the street. The officer was posting something on a pole. The car was from the same county as the Homestead boys. Scott thought the deputy might be able to help him locate the sheriff.

Scott put Sieg on a leash as he retrieved him from the car. They crossed the street to talk with the deputy. Much to Scott's surprise the deputy turned out to be Sheriff Richards. The poster displayed a photo of Adam. Sheriff Richards glanced at the boy and the dog beside him, "You must be Scott and Sieg. Sgt. Blake told me you might be showing up to help Amanda with her search. What can I do for you?"

Sieg wagged his tail as hard as he could. This man had a firm but kind voice. "I'm looking for Amanda, Sheriff Richards. Her husband, Mike wants me to keep an eye on her so she doesn't get into any trouble. Do you know where she is right now? When I called where she stayed last night she had already checked out."
Sheriff Richards replied. "Well, Scott, I'm supposed to meet her at Noon." Why don't you and that big fellow ride along with me? You can park your car in the lot next to the gas station. You can come back later with Amanda and pick it up. I've got a couple more stops to make along the way but I know exactly where we are going to meet."

Scott thought driving with the Sheriff would be quite an experience. When Sheriff Richards opened the door of the patrol car, Sieg hopped in the back seat without any command. Sheriff Richards chuckled. "Don't have to tell him what to do, do you?"

Scott climbed in the front seat beside the sheriff. "That's for sure, he's always had a mind of his own. The Sheriff pulled the patrol car onto the road and the man, boy and dog traveled down the highway.

Meanwhile at the Jacob's ranch, Sarah and the two dogs emerged from the woods and headed for the house. Sarah had enjoyed their nature walk. It had given her time to compose her anger. She began to realize during their walk in the woods that perhaps the Boxer's master was out looking him. That may be the reason the owner had not returned her call. She felt badly about not staying home to answer the phone. She hurried toward the house. She wanted to call the phone number again before her father returned at Noon. This time the Boxer's owner might be home. Sarah was still deep in thought about what she would say to the owners when she noticed a strange pickup in the barnyard. At that instant both she and Bess heard the squealing of the puppies.

Bess raced off in the direction of her young ones with Sarah fast at her heels. Bess circled the barn and was out of sight. Sarah heard Bess growl and a man's shouts, "Watch out for the dog, Jake, she's comin to defend her pups!"

Sarah rounded the corner just seconds after Bess. There before her stood two men, each holding two of Bess's puppies. Bess had seized one man by the pant leg. The man was kicking and squirming trying to loosen her grasp.

Sarah's mind began to whirl. They were stealing the puppies. These men were trying to take Bess's puppies. The gun, get the shotgun Sarah told herself and turned quickly to run to the house for the shotgun.

Just as quickly the other man dropped one of the puppies he was holding and ran after her. The man snatched Sarah by her ponytail. Sarah was jerked to the ground with a thump. As she was being dragged back to the pen she saw a station wagon pull into the barnyard. Sarah did not recognize the lady behind the wheel. Sarah did recognize the type of dogs in the back of the wagon; they were

Boxers.The Boxer, where was the Boxer? Sarah suddenly realized he was nowhere to be seen.

Amanda saw the young girl out of the corner of her eye as a man's arm reached out and grabbed the girl by her ponytail. As she stopped the car she heard the men shouting and the scream of a dog in pain. Amanda also saw the red pickup before her. Immediately she assessed the situation and reached for the gun Michael had left her. Just before he shipped overseas to Germany, Michael had taught her to use the pistol for her protection. Amanda held the gun firmly in her hand. She walked to the side of the barn. Her eyes were not prepared for such a sight. Before her she saw one of the men deliver a kick to a Collie bitch while trying to hold off the young girl. She was scratching and tearing at his face. Several Collie puppies ran about frantic, terrified.

The Collie bitch landed with a thump on the ground. She attempted to get back on her feet as one of the men approached her to deliver another kick.

Amanda found her voice. "Stop right there or I'll shoot you where you stand!"

The man turned to face her. Amanda recognized him. It was Jake Homestead! The look on his face was enough to paralyze Amanda with fear. She had never seen such hatred in a human being's face.

Amanda's hand began to shake. The gun wavered just enough to give the big man the upper hand. He lounged at Amanda, knocking the gun from her hand. Amanda tried to block her fall with her arms outstretched. She landed on the ground close to the Collie bitch. The Collie was still attempting to struggle to her feet.

Jake retrieved the gun and stood menacing above her head.

Amanda chastised herself. Why, didn't you run to the house and call the sheriff's office? Amanda knew she had been very foolish. Now everyone was in jeopardy.

Jake Homestead waved the gun about. "Well, looks like we got me a new gun and some new dogs." Marvin, bring that kickin, screamin brat over here. Let's lock her and this other lady up in the tool shed till I decide what to do with them."

Marvin Homestead didn't like the look in his brother's eye. He dare not defy him. His eyes were still black and sore from the beating he had taken from his brother after leaving the police station the other day. He wasn't about to cross his brother. He was concerned about the girl and the woman. Jake wouldn't want to leave any witnesses after getting involved with the police once already. He dropped the one remaining puppy he held in his arms. He picked Sarah up and carried her to the tool shed.

Jake grabbed Amanda by her arm and yanked her to her feet. He pushed her in the direction of the tool shed. "Get movin lady and don't try nothin else stupid. I'll shoot you and the kid right here."

Amanda steadied herself on her feet and walked to the shed. She had taken just a moment to calm the Collie bitch when she had landed at her side. Jake had forgotten about the bitch in his concern over the two hostages. Bess lay motionless tricking Jake into thinking she was dead or too severely injured to continue her attack.

Marvin had already pushed the hysterical Sarah inside the shed. Jake shoved Amanda toward the shed. She turned at the door to face Jake. "Please don't hurt us, we'll cooperate, just don't harm us or the dogs, just leave. Go away and leave us alone and we'll forget everything."

Jake knew Amanda had no intention of forgetting the whole thing. As for the dogs Jake would take what they came for. "I'll be back for you and the brat later, Lady. You can count on it." The tone of his voice revealed Jake's intentions. Amanda had no doubt; he planned to kill them both. She prayed with all her might that Sheriff Richards would arrive before these men finished their tasks outside the shed. If he didn't it would be too late. Amanda turned to Sarah. Sarah was still hysterical with anger and fright. Amanda took the girl in her arms. "You must be Sarah, my name is Amanda Nelson. I'm the lady you called about the Boxer."

Sarah collected her emotions the best she could and blurted out, "Yes I did call you, I was angry that you didn't call me back, I thought you didn't want the dog, I let my temper get away . . . "

Amanda hugged the girl tight. "It's okay, Sarah, everything will be okay. Sheriff Richards will be here soon, he knows I was coming here to find Adam."

"Adam, so that's his name," Sarah declared.

In unison they both exclaimed, "Where is he?" In just a few seconds they both realized they had not seen Adam at all during the scuffle. Sarah had not seen Adam since they ran toward the house. Amanda had not seen him at all when she pulled into the barnyard. Both the girl and the woman suddenly found themselves more troubled about the fate of Adam, Bess and the puppies than their own safety. What would those men do to the dogs and puppies? Amanda remembered Melody and Abby too. She had left them crated in the car. Again she prayed. "Oh God, send Sheriff Richards quickly, please."

If they could get free, both Amanda and Sarah were prepared to fight for the lives of their dogs. Amanda feared for their lives too. She could not convey her fears to Sarah. She would have to keep her conclusion of what Jake Homestead would do with them in the back of her mind. Amanda felt her unborn child move inside her. It would be difficult but Amanda prepared to fight with all her strength to protect the dogs, Sarah and her unborn child. She had weakened once and allowed Jake to take the gun from her. The next time she had the chance she would not back down.

Chapter 19 -

Adam's Vengeance

$\mathcal{A}$dam had run toward the house with the girl and the Collie. When he had reached the barnyard he froze in his tracks. Before him was the pickup truck he had feared would find him ever since his escape. He glanced at the cages in the back of the truck. He could see a large black dog. At that instant he had heard the men's' voices and had run for safety inside the barn. He stood in the corner of one of the stalls trembling with fear. Adam heard another vehicle drive into the barnyard. He did not dare show himself.

Adam heard the girl's screams and Bess's cries. Adam thought he had heard another familiar voice, the voice of his mistress. At the thought of her, Adam's fears diminished a little. He could not be sure that was her voice. He crept slowly toward the barn door to investigate. He reached the door in time to see one of the men slam the door on the tool shed. His mistress and Sarah were nowhere in sight. Adam recognized the station wagon parked in the barnyard. It was his car! The driver's door hung open. Adam could see his mother and sister inside their crates. Oh how he wanted to run to the car. The men stood between him and the safety of the car.

Adam slipped back into the barn. He would wait for his chance to run to the car. From his vantage point Adam watched as the men gathered up the Collie's puppies. They locked them into a cage next to the black dog. The puppies were crying. Adam looked around. Bess was nowhere in sight. He remembered her running to the side of the barn to the puppy pen. He had heard her cries of pain. Adam wandered to the back of the barn seeking another way out. He walked into the feed room. There he discovered a window open. Adam jumped up on the feed bin and peered out the window. He saw Bess lying on her side, panting and trying valiantly to get to her feet. She would still try to defend her little ones and Sarah. Adam wanted to go to the Bess. His fear of the men was still too great. Adam could see the men more clearly now from this window.

The big man, Adam hated and feared the most. He threw something on the seat of the station wagon and he rounded up the remainder of the puppies. He put them in the cage. He ordered, Marvin. "Go get them two bitches out of the back of the station wagon and put them in with the pups. We can use them for breedin."

Adam saw the smaller man move toward the rear of the station wagon. He could hear Harmony and Abby barking a warning at the man to keep away from their property.

Adam watched as the big man went back to the door of the shed and unlocked the door. "Bring me that gun when you get done with that and we'll finish this."

It was then Adam heard his mistress scream. "No" The huge man reached inside the door and dragged Amanda into Adam's view. At that instant Adam's fear gave way. His instincts to protect his mistress were aroused. Adam leapt from the window. He closed the distance between him and the big man in a few short seconds. The force of the Adam's impact knocked the big man to the ground. Adam was upon him locking his deathlike grip at the man's throat. The man only had time to yell one word, "Marvin!" Adam held on to the man's throat. He did not tear or shake. He tightened his grip as the man fought to break him away. Adam held his grip like his ancient ancestors must have gripped the throat of the bulls they were trained to control.

Amanda and Sarah stood by for only a moment. Their surprise of seeing Adam gave way to the necessity of assisting Adam in his battle. Amanda picked up a shovel from inside the shed while Sarah ran for the house, "I'll get the shotgun," she shouted.

Meanwhile, Marvin had trouble of his own. As he reached into the crate to grab Harmony she lunged at him. She snapped at his hand. Harmony did not know this stranger. He had no business reaching into her crate. The sound of distress in her mistress's voice also excited her. Her teeth hit home at least once as the blood rushed from Marvin's finger.

Jake's scream distracted Marvin just long enough. Harmony took the opportunity to free herself from the crate. She then gripped his leg with her mouth.

Bess had finally struggled to her feet. She went to the boxer bitch's aid and attached herself to one of his arms. Sarah raced to the house and back. She carried the loaded shotgun in her arms. Marvin struggled to reach the gun Jake had thrown on the seat of the station wagon. It was a difficult task with the two dogs firmly attached to his arm and leg. Just as Marvin reached for the gun inside the station wagon Sarah approached his side. "Touch it and your dead." Sarah's voice showed no signs of apprehension. Marvin was sure she would pull the trigger. He backed away with Harmony still firmly attached to his pant leg and Bess on his arm. "Get over to the tool shed," Sarah ordered.

Amanda stopped pounding Jake with the shovel. She saw Sarah had Marvin in tow. Jake had stopped struggling. He was still alive but he had lost his determination to continue the fight. Sarah called to Bess and the Collie let go of Marvin's leg. Harmony too released her hold on Marvin and trotted to Amanda's side when she called. Only Adam held his grip, he would not let go!

Chapter 20 -

More Help Arrives

$\mathcal{S}$heriff Richards, Scott and Sieg arrived in town shortly before 11:00 that morning. The sheriff knew he was early for his appointment with Amanda. He would take a little time for a cup of coffee and another visit around town with the locals. This would be a good opportunity to introduce Scott and Sieg to some local people. Since Sieg was a perfect example of the dog they were searching for, the posters would not be necessary.

After parking the patrol car outside the grocery store, Sheriff Richards led Scott and Sieg toward the café. He was just about to take his first sip of coffee when Ben Ford walked into the café.

"Hey, Sheriff, I got a message for you from a little lady named Amanda."

Sheriff Richards put his cup down. "You mean she's already been in town? We weren't supposed to meet until Noon."

"Don't know nothin about your schedule, Sheriff,. All I know is she said she knew where her dog was. Said for you to meet her there."

"Well, where is she?", Sheriff Richard asked.

"She went to Tim Jacob's place," Ben replied.

Sheriff Richards put a quarter down on the counter to pay for his coffee, and turned to Scott. "We better get on out there and see what's going on. Tim Jacobs sure isn't a dog thief." They hurried back to the patrol car. The sheriff radioed his dispatcher that he was headed for the Jacobs place. As they drove toward the ranch they came up behind Tim Jacob's pickup. Sheriff Richards figured Tim had been out running errands. He followed Tim down the highway. When Tim made the turn into the long driveway Sheriff Richards was still right behind.

Tim stopped the pickup just beyond the cattle guard. He got out of the truck and walked back to the Sheriff's car, "What's going on Matt, was I speeding?"

Sheriff Richards grinned. "Nope, just coming to check on whether a lady showed up at your place looking for a Boxer."

Tim answered. "Don't think so. We have a Boxer though. Been around here a week or so. He just wandered in one day. Sarah took it under her wing. You know how she is about strays? We've been trying to get in touch with the owners. When I left for the fair this morning they still hadn't called. I've been waiting to talk to you about it." Tim noticed Sieg and Scott in the car, "Hey, who are your friends, Matt? That dog there could be a dead ringer for the one at my place. This one's a little older but almost exactly like the one at the house."

Scott chimed in. "Sieg is Adam's father. I'm a friend of Adam's owner.

Sheriff Richards explained further. "They haven't been calling because the dog's owner has been tearing up the countryside looking for him. Seems dog fighters stole him. You know the Homestead boys?"

Tim shuddered at the sound of their name. "Come on up to the house, Matt. We'll see if she's there yet. We left Sarah at home this morning to keep trying the phone number. Chances are your lady has been and gone by now."

"I don't think so," Sheriff Richards replied. "She left a message for me with Ben Ford to meet her at your place. She's probably visiting with Sarah."

Tim got back into his pickup. Sheriff Richards drove the patrol car behind him. No one, not Tim Jacobs, the Sheriff or Scott were prepared for what they were about to behold. Tim knew something was wrong the minute he saw the red pickup truck. It belonged to the Homestead boys.

Sheriff Richards quickly came to the same conclusion. Both men slammed on the brakes of their vehicles and jumped out, Scott and Sieg were right behind. They all observed the bed of the pickup filled with cages. The cages were filled with Collie puppies and a big black dog. The scene was chaotic at best.

Frantically they searched for signs of Sarah and Amanda. Just beyond the pickup was the station wagon. Beyond that they spied

Sarah with the shotgun pointed at Marvin Homestead. Marvin stood in the doorway of the tool shed. On the ground lay Jake Homestead, a Boxer still gripping his throat. Next to Sarah stood Amanda, Bess and another Boxer.

Sheriff Richards drew his gun. He approached Marvin and hand cuffed him. Tim walked to his daughter's side, reached over and took the shotgun from Sarah's hands. "It's okay, Pumpkin, we'll take care of it from here."

Only then did Sarah allow herself to tremble. They were safe now. All of them were safe.

Scott approached Amanda and put his arm around her. She was trembling too.

Sheriff Richards secured Marvin in the back of his car. Sieg, hackles raised, stood guard at the car door while the sheriff radioed headquarters for back up. Then he walked over to Amanda and Jake. "Okay, Amanda, you can call off your boy now. I think old Jake's had enough."

Amanda turned to Adam, "Okay, Adam, it's okay, let go."

Adam held tight and did not let go. The rage inside him had been stored for a long time. His anger was fueled by a stronger nature, the instinct to survive.

Again Amanda tried to make him give up his grip. Still he clung to the man's throat. Adam had never refused Amanda's commands. She sensed, however, that it would take some doing to bring her Adam back.

Scott tried to calm Adam too. He had never seen such hatred in any Boxer before.

Sheriff Richards cautioned. "If he doesn't let go soon, Amanda, he's going to kill Jake. You know I can't let that happen. I won't have any choice. I'll have to shoot him if you don't get him off."

Amanda, Scott and Sarah all echoed the same words, "No, give us another chance to get him off." Amanda begged. "He saved our lives. They were going to kill us."

Tim stepped up to the sheriff's side. "Matt, let them have their chance. He saved my baby's life. I won't let you shoot him over a man like Jake Homestead."

Sheriff Richards knew how they all felt. He knew too it was his duty to protect all the citizens of his county. That included Jake Homestead. "All right I'll give him another chance, Tim. But that's it. I cannot not allow him to kill Jake although it would certainly serve him right."

Amanda knelt beside Adam. She began to stroke him softly on the head. Sarah followed suit. She began to caress the dog with her gentle touch. Eventually Amanda's soft voice and Sarah's soft hands began to work their spell. Like his father before him, Adam had been raised with love. That love would bring him back to reality.

Amanda, Scott and Sarah stood back. They watched as the crazed animal gradually returned to the Adam they all loved. Adam released his death grip on Jake's throat. He whimpered as he turned to lick Amanda's face.

Jake Homestead rolled away. He slithered in the dirt like a wounded animal. An animal was a good description for him. Sieg immediately took a stance over Jake. Jake's eyes filled with terror again. Sieg supervised Sheriff Richard's every move as he placed the handcuffs on Jake and helped him to the patrol car.

This time the Homestead boys had met their match. A pregnant woman, a girl and three dogs had been their waterloo.

Chapter 21 -

Sad Farewells - Cheerful Salutations

Amanda and her Boxers spent that night in the comfort of the Jacobs' guest room. Sheriff Richards drove Scott and Sieg back to Scott's car. Scott and Sieg returned home to tell everyone the good news. Everyone agreed that Amanda needed to rest before attempting the drive home. She and Adam napped the rest of the day, snuggled together in Sarah's bed. The ordeal was finally over. Both Adam and Amanda were safe in the solace of the Jacobs' home.

Later, Amanda and Sarah spent much of the night talking and sharing their stories about Adam. They wondered about his quest to find his mistress and home. If only he could talk, what stories would he tell? Amanda shared stories of Adam's accomplishments in the show ring. She also told Sarah the wonderful story of Sieg and Scott.

Adam felt completely safe at last. He was content, curled up between Amanda and Sarah on the sofa. Harmony and Abby laid at their feet.

Bess would spend the night at Dr. Hager's house. She had not been seriously injured. Just in case, Dr. Hager wanted to keep her overnight for observation in the event there was any internal bleeding. The puppies were none the worse for their experience. After Sarah fed them their dinner, they all cuddled up in their usual pile in barn stall.

Sheriff Richards had taken the Rottweiler back to his office. There he would attempt to find his owner.

The next morning Amanda and her Boxers left for home. Sarah could not hide the tears as Adam took his place beside Amanda in the car. Sarah knew Adam belonged with Amanda, yet Adam had also claimed a large piece of Sarah's heart.

Amanda's eyes also welled up with tears. "I'll write as soon as we're settled in Germany, Sarah. I promise the minute we get back to the States we'll all come for a visit, me, Adam, the girls, Michael and, of course, the new baby. Bless you for taking care of Adam. I know he and I will never forget you. Take care of your Bess and we'll see you again."

By now Sarah could only give a brave smile. She hugged Amanda and Adam. She watched until the station wagon was out of sight. The tears rolled from her eyes like a river.

Tim Jacobs took his daughter in his arms. "Come on Pumpkin, let's go get your Bess."

One week later Amanda, Adam, Harmony and Abby left for Germany. Dr. Stockman had given Adam a thorough exam. Although he was still under weight his physical condition was improving. Adam was fit to travel.

Scott and Sieg drove Amanda and the dogs to the airport for their departure. The goodbyes did not come easy for them; however, they knew it was not a forever goodbye. Amanda promised to be back for Scott's high school graduation. "See you," were the last words Scott spoke to Amanda.

Amanda watched from the window of the plane as the pair, dog and boy stood watching. Friends like this were indeed forever.

Several months passed. Sarah searched the mailbox everyday for a letter from Amanda. Just before Thanksgiving the long awaited letter arrived. Inside the letter was a photograph, a family portrait of Amanda, Michael, Harmony, Abby, Adam and the new baby. Sarah unfolded the letter. She read.

Dear Sarah & Bess,

I am sorry for taking so long to write. The move to Frankfort was hectic. We did arrive safely and Adam and the girls have adjusted to our new house quite well. As you can see by the photo our new "addition" arrived on October 31st and now we have our own little "Pumpkin" as your father calls you. Also in your honor we have called the baby "Sarah," somehow the name seemed to fit quite well.

You will be pleased to know that Adam has recovered completely from his wounds and although he is still uncomfortable around strangers he becomes more like his old self every day. When I talk to the baby at the sound of the name "Sarah" he picks up his ears and wags his tail. He has not forgotten you.

Thank you so much for the photo of you and Bess. I am happy she has recovered from her ordeal. Your photo reminds me daily of how wonderful you and your Bess were to my Adam.

I received a letter from Sheriff Richards a few weeks ago and have forwarded my affidavit for the Homestead's trial. The value of Adam, the Rottweiler and Bess's puppies was more than enough to charge them with a Felony Theft. If all goes well they will spend a good deal of time behind bars. Sheriff Richards also told me your Dad had helped to locate the area where they were keeping the other stolen dogs. I was pleased those dogs had been rescued too.

Be sure and thank you father too for the help with your State Legislature in getting legislation started to outlaw dog fighting in your state. Maybe by the time the Homesteads get back out of jail the new law will be on the books. Sheriff Richards told me Jake Homestead would have a permanent scar to remind him of his encounter with Adam. That should serve to remind him, and others like him, that horrible deeds can come back to haunt you.

I hope you and your family have a lovely holiday season. I shall write more at Christmas. If all goes well we should all be back home sometime next fall.

All our love,
Amanda, Michael, Sarah, the girls and of course, Adam

Sarah carried the letter into her father's office and allowed him to read it.

Tim Jacobs just beamed. "Well, Pumpkin, you've got yourself a namesake now for sure. But there's only one Sarah for me." Tim reached out and hugged his daughter. "You better get busy with your chores. I better get back to the bill paying before your Mama gives us both heck."

Sarah put the letter in her pocket. She would read it again later.

The Christmas holidays brought a Christmas card and another letter from Amanda. This time she wrote that Adam had made quite a sensation with the local Germans. The distinguished ancestors in Adam and Sieg's pedigree had not been forgotten. Some breeders had solicited Adam's stud service. He had been bred to several bitches in the area. Soon there would be more little Adams or Siegs walking about. Sarah smiled at the thought of Adam as a puppy. He must have been a grand little fellow.

In February the Homesteads stood trial and were convicted of Grand Theft. They were sentenced to five years in prison. Sarah and her father attended the trial.

Sarah saw first hand the scar Jake Homestead still bore on his neck. His appearance and attitude in the courtroom left her and her father little doubt that Jake had been shaken by his encounter. The rasp in Jake's voice would serve to remind him for the rest of his life of the Boxer who so valiantly fought to protect those he loved. Love always wins over fear and intimidation.

The end of March brought signs of spring. Tim Jacobs busied himself with the new foals being born almost every night. They had increased the size of their herd considerably. As usual Sarah stayed at her father's side. The wonders of birth never ceased to amaze her.

Another long night in the barn the night before had left Sarah and her father exhausted. After the early morning chores were done, they headed for the house for some breakfast.

A delivery truck pulled into the barnyard. The deliveryman parked the van and called. "I've got a delivery here for a Sarah Jacobs."

Sarah knew her birthday was close. She figured her Mom had ordered her the pretty party dress she had so admired in the Penny's catalog. "I'm Sarah Jacobs," she informed the driver. The driver handed her his clipboard. "Sign on the last line while I unload the crate."

Sarah looked at her father in bewilderment. "What kind of dress comes in a crate?" Tim Jacobs tried hard not to let a smile give away any surprise. He knew full well what Sarah was about to receive. "Beats me, Pumpkin, just sign the darn paper and let's see."

The driver appeared from behind the van carrying the crate. It was an animal crate. From inside came the sounds of a puppy struggling to free itself from confinement. The driver placed the crate on the ground. "There you go. This crate came all the way from Germany."

"Germany!" Sarah exclaimed. Attached to the crate was a note. Sarah took it and handed it to her father. "Read it to me, Daddy, while I get this little guy out."

Sarah could see it was a Boxer puppy. He was fawn like Adam. Tim Jacobs read the note.

Dear Sarah:

Just a little something for your birthday next week; Adam and I wanted you to have him. His name is Baron and he is Adam's son. You and Bess take good care of him. Adam and I will come by and check on him in September after we get back home.

God bless,
Amanda and Adam

Sarah held the fidgeting puppy in her arms. She smiled through her tears of joy. "Hello, Baron, welcome home." Sarah's soothing voice and gentle hands worked their magic on the puppy much like they had on his father. Baron was secure. His quest for his mistress was over too

Acknowledgments

$\mathcal{I}$ would like to thank the following organizations for their commitment in fighting breed specific legislation and their efforts to preserve the rights of dog owners and their canine companions. If you desire information on legislation in your area, I urge you to contact these organizations.

The National Breed Clubs Alliance
1005 Mt. Simon Drive
Livermore, CO 80586

The American Boxer Club
C/o Sandy Orr, Secretary
7706 North 57th Street
Omaha, NE 68152

American Kennel Club
51 Madison Avenue
New York, NY 10010

National Animal Interest Alliance
PO Box 66579
Portland, Oregon 97290-6579

American Dog Owners Association
P. O. Box 41194
Fredericksburg, VA 22402